Gertrude Chandler Warner's

THE BOXCAR CHILDREN GRAPHIC NOVELS

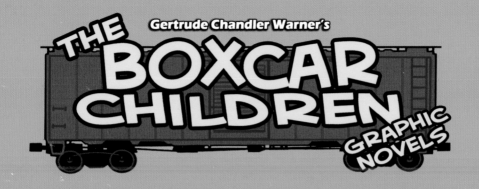

BOOK SIX

BLUE BAY MYSTERY

Henry, Jessie, Violet, and Benny are in for a surprise when their Grandfather arranges to take them on a special trip to a deserted South Seas island. Along with a sailor named Lars and their old friend Mike Wood, the Aldens set sail for adventure.

But when they arrive on the island, their rustic adventure leads to the discovery that Blue Bay Island holds a mystery and it's up to the Aldens to solve it!

THE BOXCAR CHILDREN
GRAPHIC NOVELS

1. THE BOXCAR CHILDREN
2. SURPRISE ISLAND
3. THE YELLOW HOUSE MYSTERY
4. MYSTERY RANCH
5. MIKE'S MYSTERY
6. BLUE BAY MYSTERY

Gertrude Chandler Warner's

THE BOXCAR CHILDREN
BLUE BAY MYSTERY

Adapted by Rob M. Worley
Illustrated by Mark Bloodworth

Henry Alden

Jessie Alden

Watch

Violet Alden

Benny Alden

magic
Wagon

Visit us at www.abdopublishing.com

Published by Magic Wagon, a division of the ABDO Group, 8000 West 78th Street, Edina, Minnesota 55439.

Adapted by Rob M. Worley
Illustrated by Mark Bloodworth
Colored by Wes Hartman
Lettered by Johnny Lowe
Edited by Stephanie Hedlund
Interior layout and design by Kristen Fitzner Denton
Cover art by Mike Dubisch
Book design and packaging by Shannon Eric Denton

Library of Congress Cataloging-in-Publication Data

Worley, Rob M.
Blue Bay mystery / adapted by Rob M. Worley ; illustrated by Mark Bloodworth.
p. cm. -- (Gertrude Chandler Warner's boxcar children)
ISBN 978-1-60270-591-3
[1. Orphans--Fiction. 2. Family life--Fiction. 3. Mystery and detective stories.]
I. Bloodworth, Mark, ill. II. Warner, Gertrude Chandler, 1890-1979. Blue Bay mystery. III. Title.
PZ7.W887625Blu 2009
[E]--dc22
2008036098

Printed in the United States of America, North Mankato, Minnesota
122009
012009

BOOK SIX

BLUE BAY MYSTERY

Contents

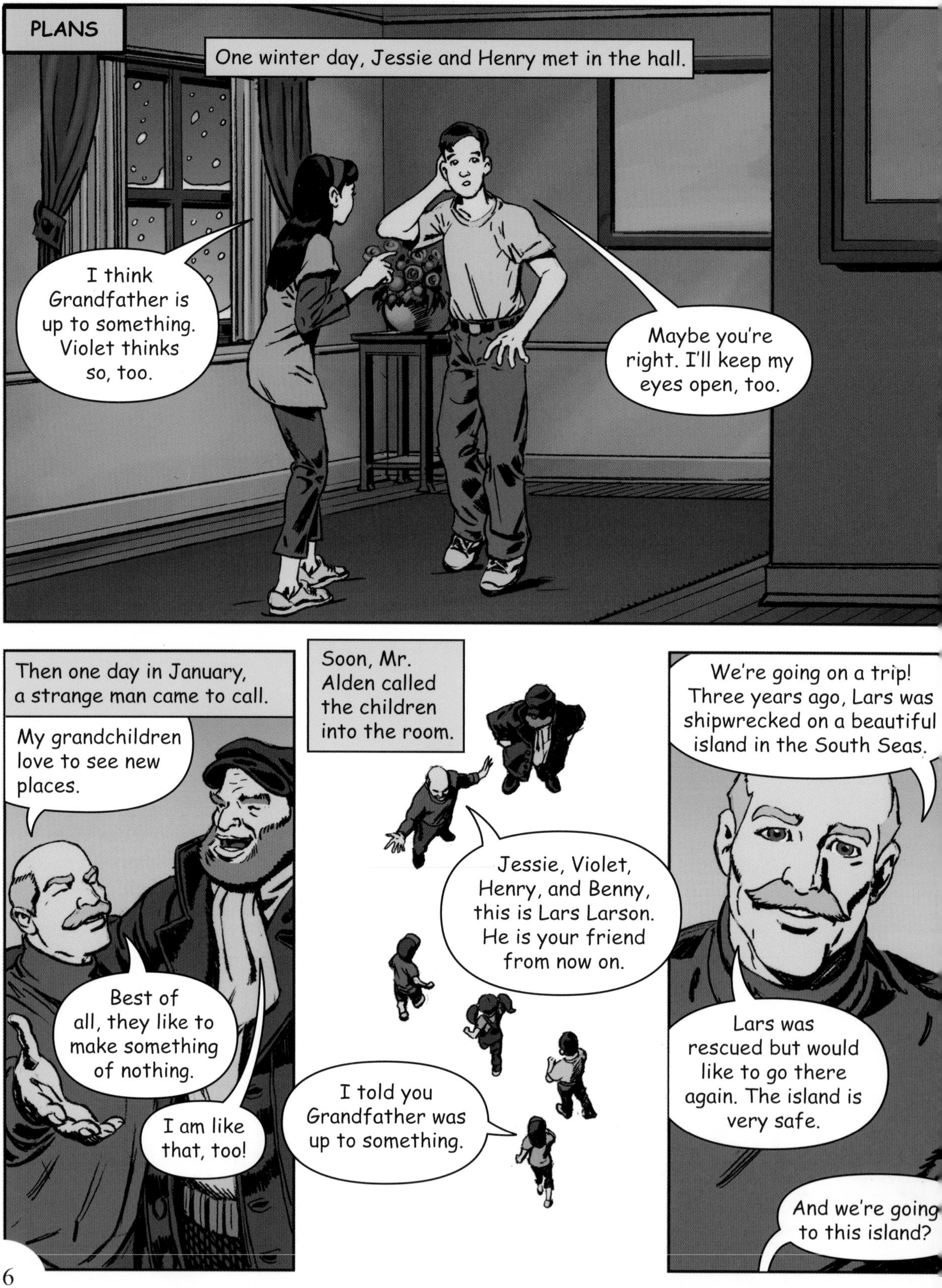
PLANS
One winter day, Jessie and Henry met in the hall.
I think Grandfather is up to something. Violet thinks so, too.
Maybe you're right. I'll keep my eyes open, too.
Then one day in January, a strange man came to call.
My grandchildren love to see new places.
Best of all, they like to make something of nothing.
I am like that, too!
Soon, Mr. Alden called the children into the room.
Jessie, Violet, Henry, and Benny, this is Lars Larson. He is your friend from now on.
I told you Grandfather was up to something.
We're going on a trip! Three years ago, Lars was shipwrecked on a beautiful island in the South Seas.
Lars was rescued but would like to go there again. The island is very safe.
And we're going to this island?

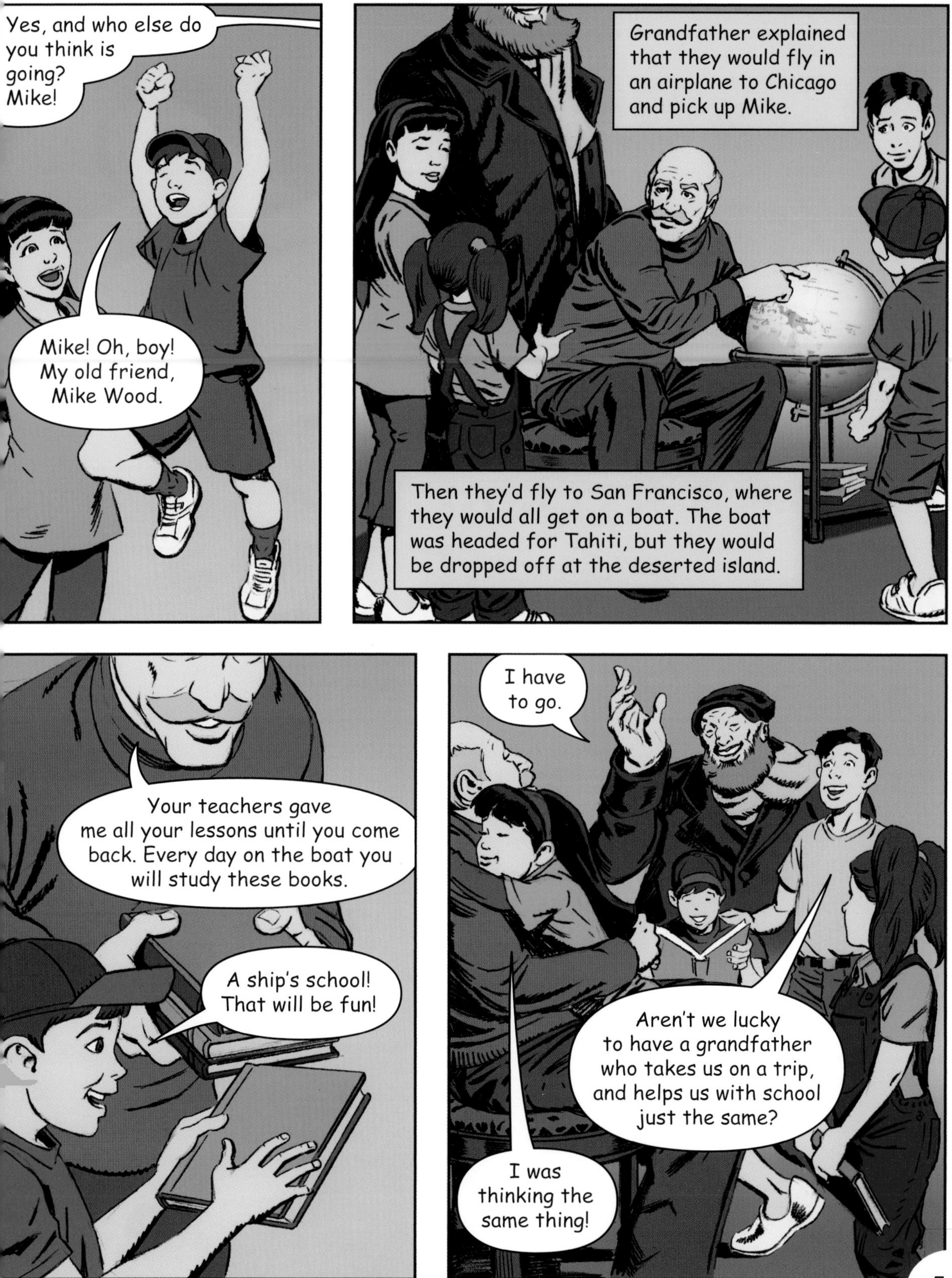
Yes, and who else do you think is going? Mike!
Mike! Oh, boy! My old friend, Mike Wood.
Grandfather explained that they would fly in an airplane to Chicago and pick up Mike.
Then they'd fly to San Francisco, where they would all get on a boat. The boat was headed for Tahiti, but they would be dropped off at the deserted island.
Your teachers gave me all your lessons until you come back. Every day on the boat you will study these books.
A ship's school! That will be fun!
I have to go.
Aren't we lucky to have a grandfather who takes us on a trip, and helps us with school just the same?
I was thinking the same thing!

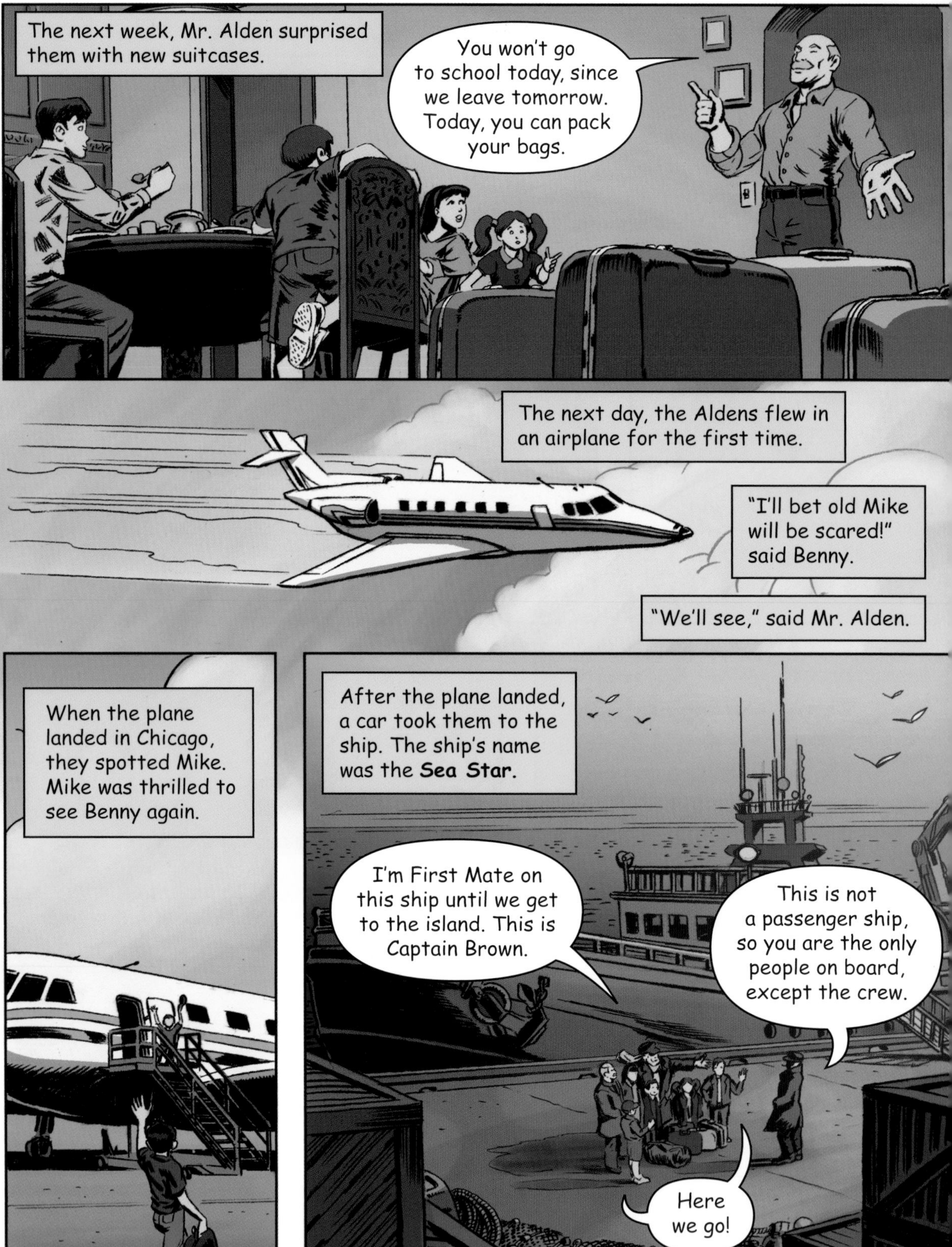
The next week, Mr. Alden surprised them with new suitcases.
You won't go to school today, since we leave tomorrow. Today, you can pack your bags.
The next day, the Aldens flew in an airplane for the first time.
"I'll bet old Mike will be scared!" said Benny.
"We'll see," said Mr. Alden.
When the plane landed in Chicago, they spotted Mike. Mike was thrilled to see Benny again.
After the plane landed, a car took them to the ship. The ship's name was the **Sea Star**.
I'm First Mate on this ship until we get to the island. This is Captain Brown.
This is not a passenger ship, so you are the only people on board, except the crew.
Here we go!

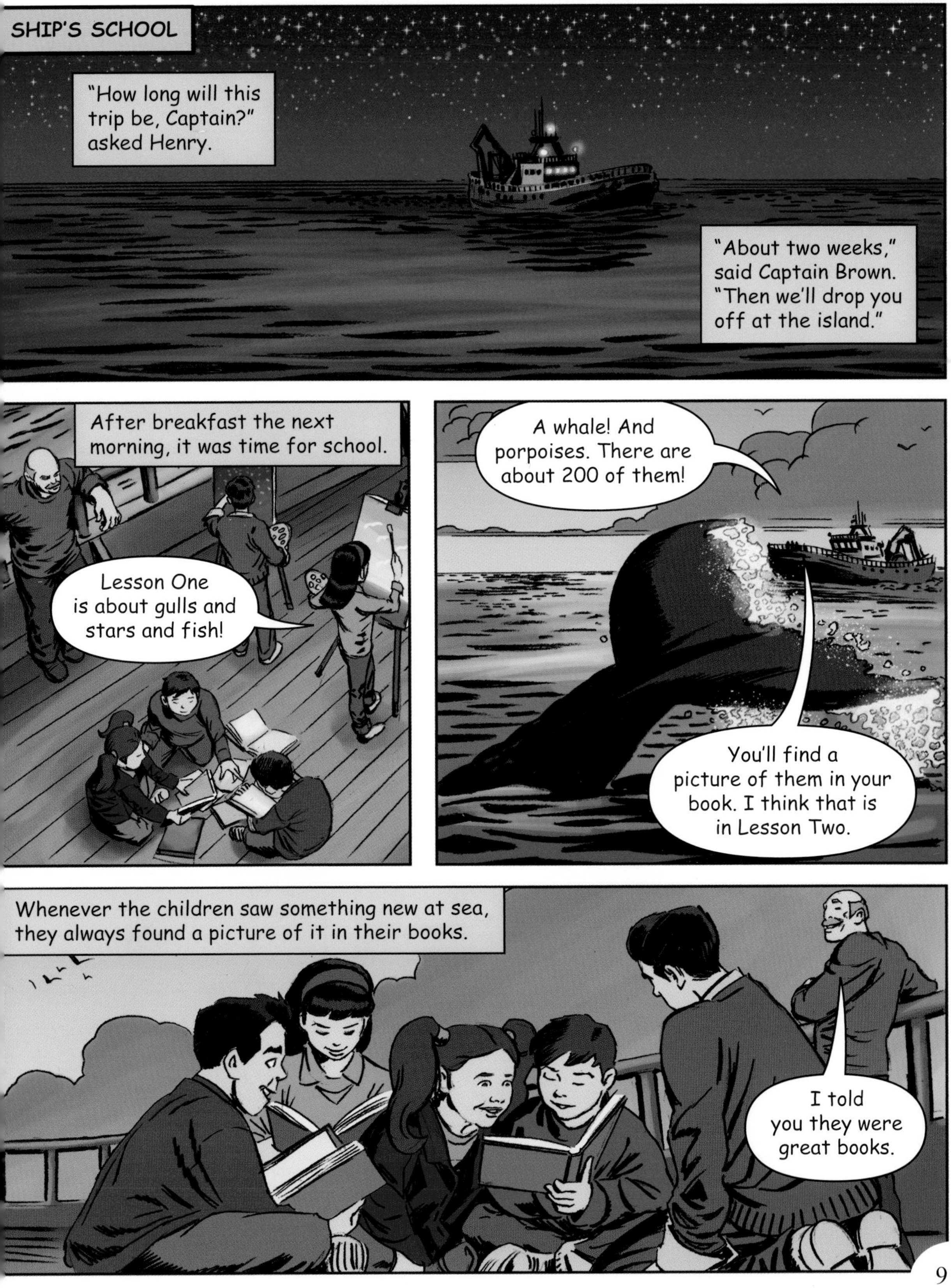
SHIP'S SCHOOL
"How long will this trip be, Captain?" asked Henry.
"About two weeks," said Captain Brown. "Then we'll drop you off at the island."
After breakfast the next morning, it was time for school.
Lesson One is about gulls and stars and fish!
A whale! And porpoises. There are about 200 of them!
You'll find a picture of them in your book. I think that is in Lesson Two.
Whenever the children saw something new at sea, they always found a picture of it in their books.
I told you they were great books.

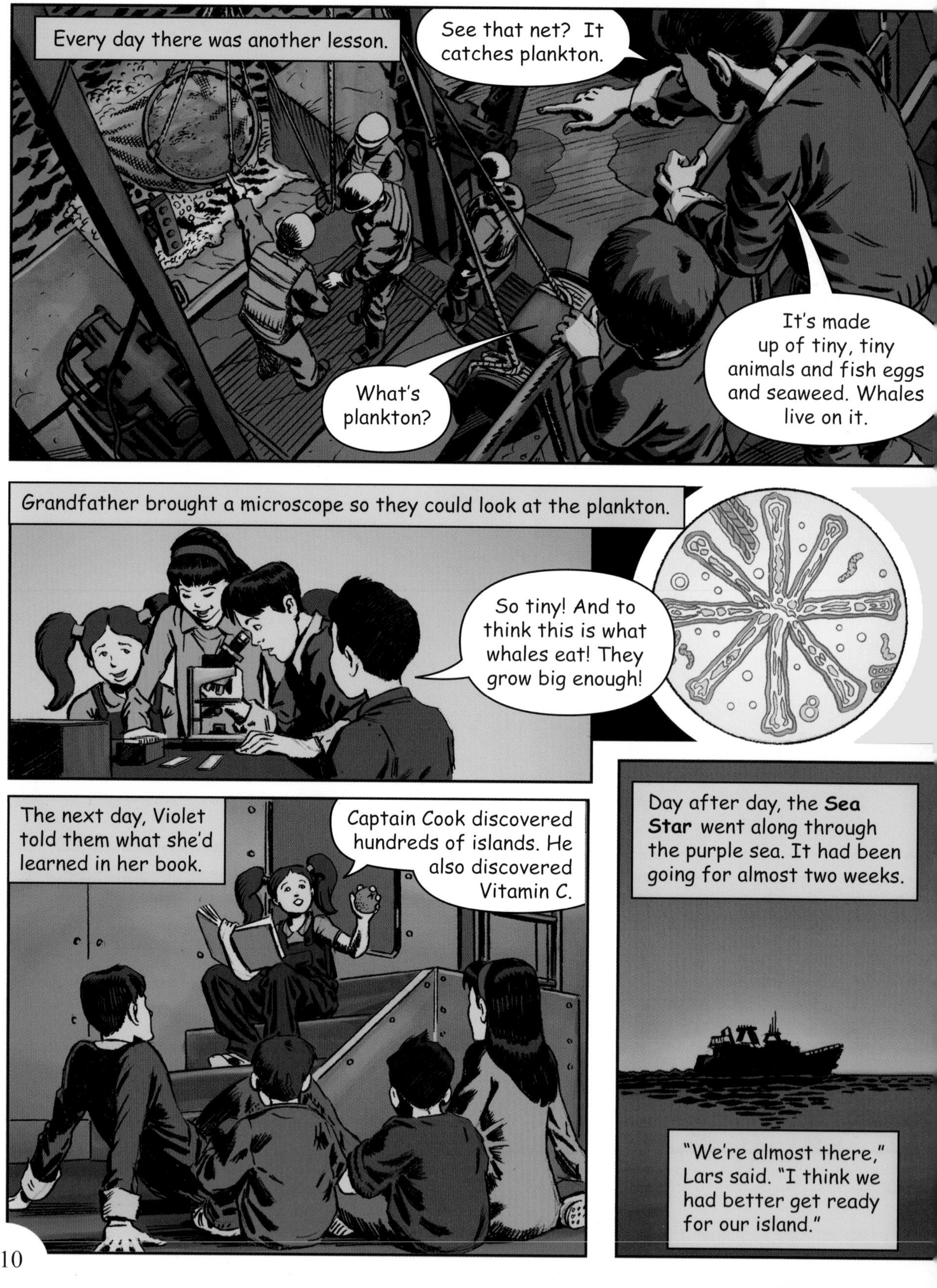
Every day there was another lesson.
See that net? It catches plankton.
What's plankton?
It's made up of tiny, tiny animals and fish eggs and seaweed. Whales live on it.
Grandfather brought a microscope so they could look at the plankton.
So tiny! And to think this is what whales eat! They grow big enough!
The next day, Violet told them what she'd learned in her book.
Captain Cook discovered hundreds of islands. He also discovered Vitamin C.
Day after day, the **Sea Star** went along through the purple sea. It had been going for almost two weeks.
"We're almost there," Lars said. "I think we had better get ready for our island."

THE LIFEBOAT

Be sure to wear good shoes. You'll be walking over sharp stones and shells.

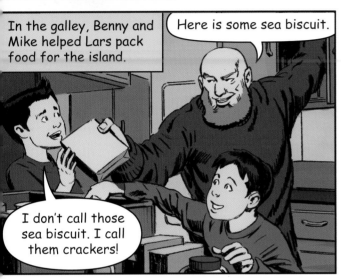

In the galley, Benny and Mike helped Lars pack food for the island.

Here is some sea biscuit.

I don't call those sea biscuit. I call them crackers!

Matches.

Good! We'll need a fire.

They went to the deck, knowing they would soon see the island. Lars spotted the island first, but waited to see who would be the next to see it.

Is that land, Lars, or is it nothing?

It's land, Henry. Soon we will see the green palm trees and the big round bay.

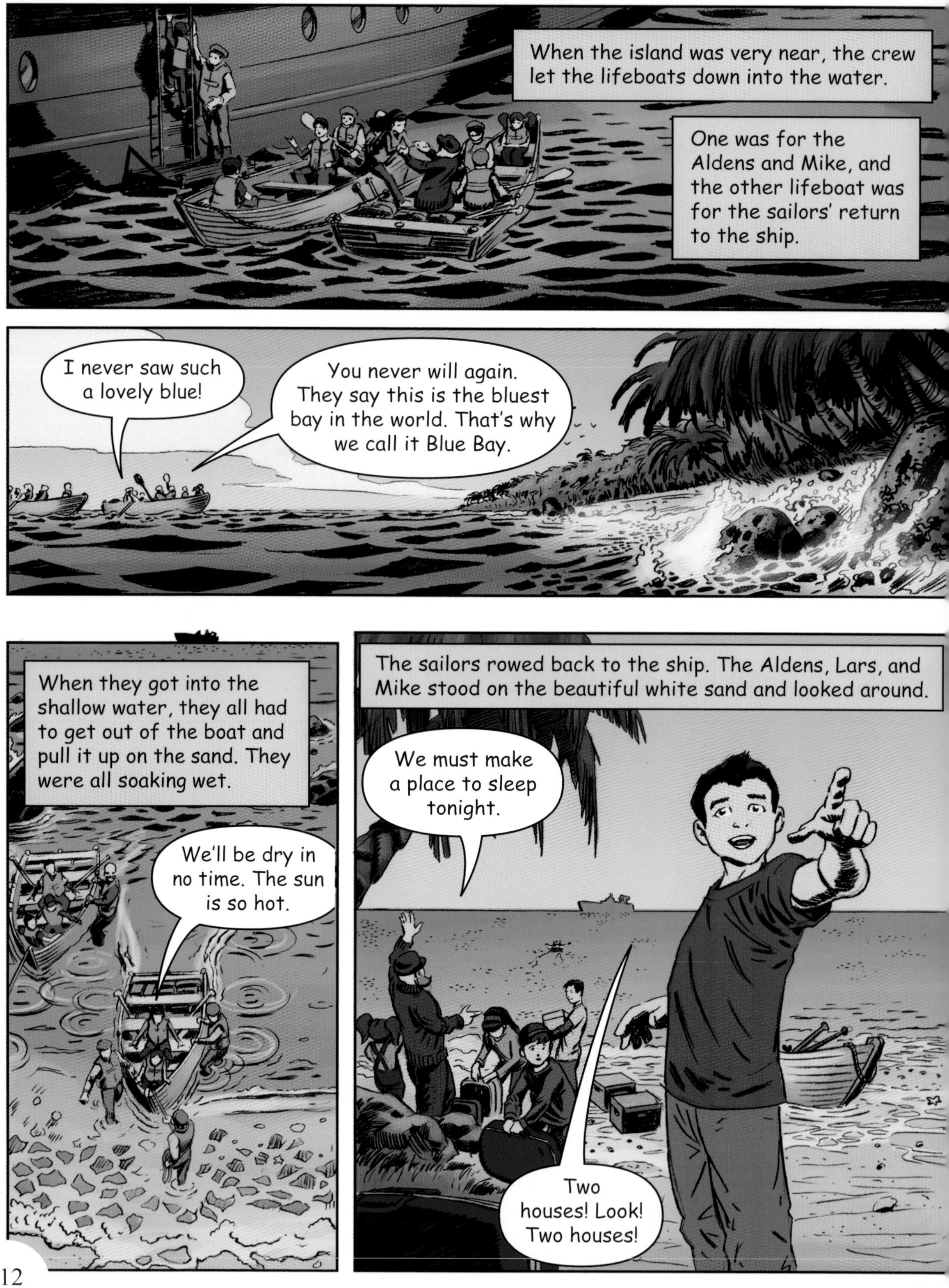
When the island was very near, the crew let the lifeboats down into the water.
One was for the Aldens and Mike, and the other lifeboat was for the sailors' return to the ship.
I never saw such a lovely blue!
You never will again. They say this is the bluest bay in the world. That's why we call it Blue Bay.
When they got into the shallow water, they all had to get out of the boat and pull it up on the sand. They were all soaking wet.
We'll be dry in no time. The sun is so hot.
The sailors rowed back to the ship. The Aldens, Lars, and Mike stood on the beautiful white sand and looked around.
We must make a place to sleep tonight.
Two houses! Look! Two houses!

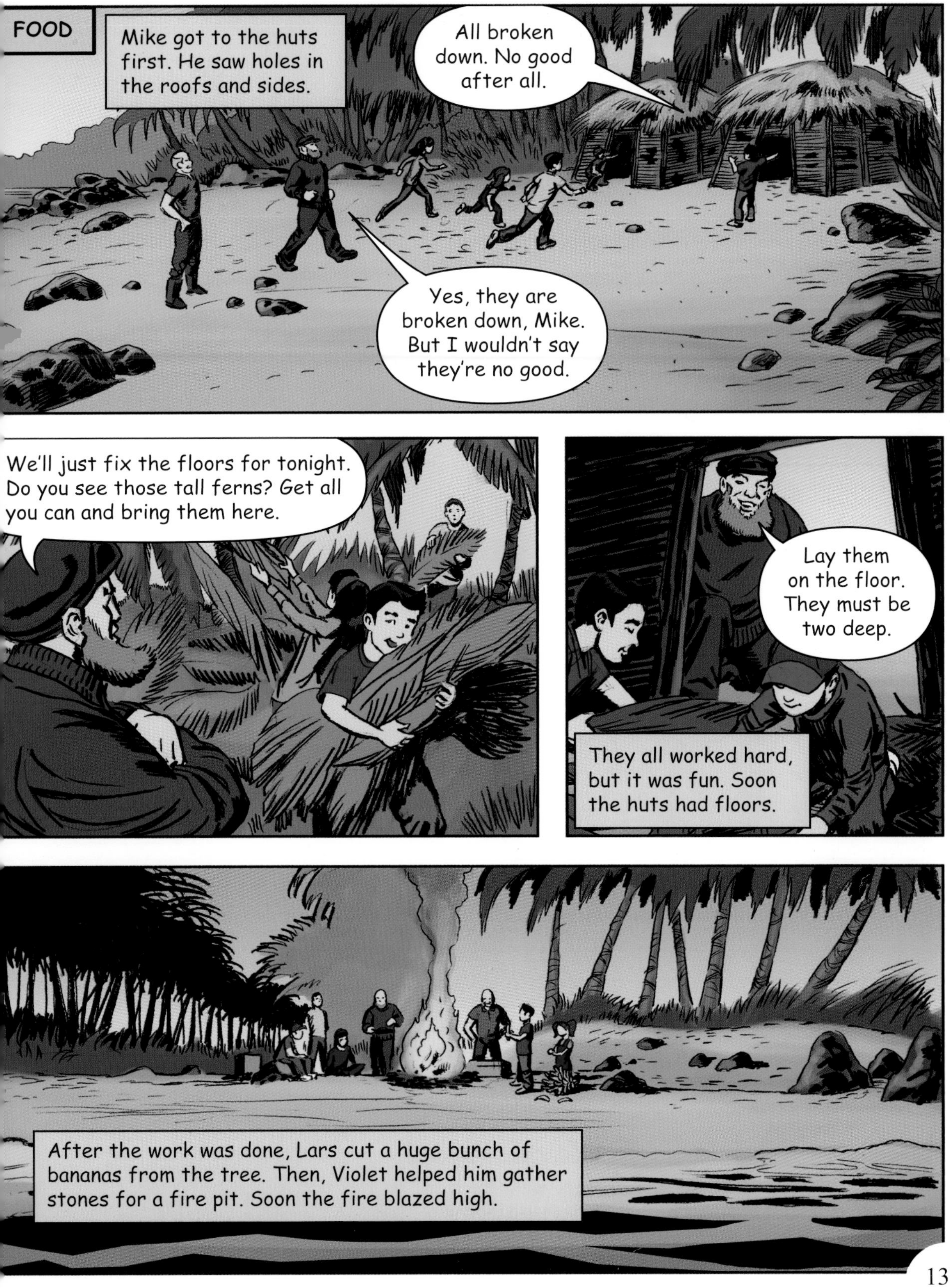
FOOD
Mike got to the huts first. He saw holes in the roofs and sides.
All broken down. No good after all.
Yes, they are broken down, Mike. But I wouldn't say they're no good.
We'll just fix the floors for tonight. Do you see those tall ferns? Get all you can and bring them here.
Lay them on the floor. They must be two deep.
They all worked hard, but it was fun. Soon the huts had floors.
After the work was done, Lars cut a huge bunch of bananas from the tree. Then, Violet helped him gather stones for a fire pit. Soon the fire blazed high.

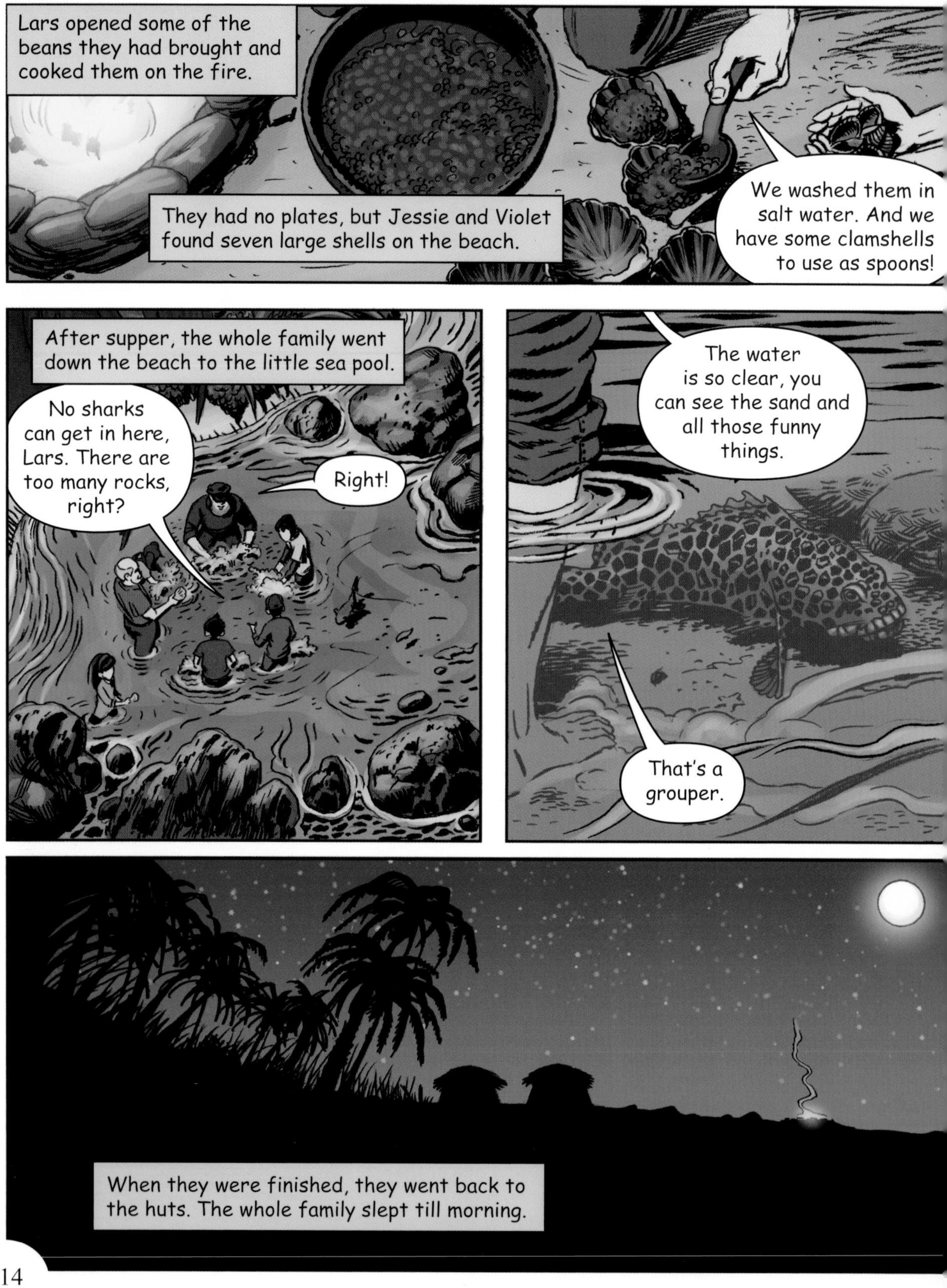

Lars opened some of the beans they had brought and cooked them on the fire.
They had no plates, but Jessie and Violet found seven large shells on the beach.
We washed them in salt water. And we have some clamshells to use as spoons!
After supper, the whole family went down the beach to the little sea pool.
No sharks can get in here, Lars. There are too many rocks, right?
Right!
The water is so clear, you can see the sand and all those funny things.
That's a grouper.
When they were finished, they went back to the huts. The whole family slept till morning.

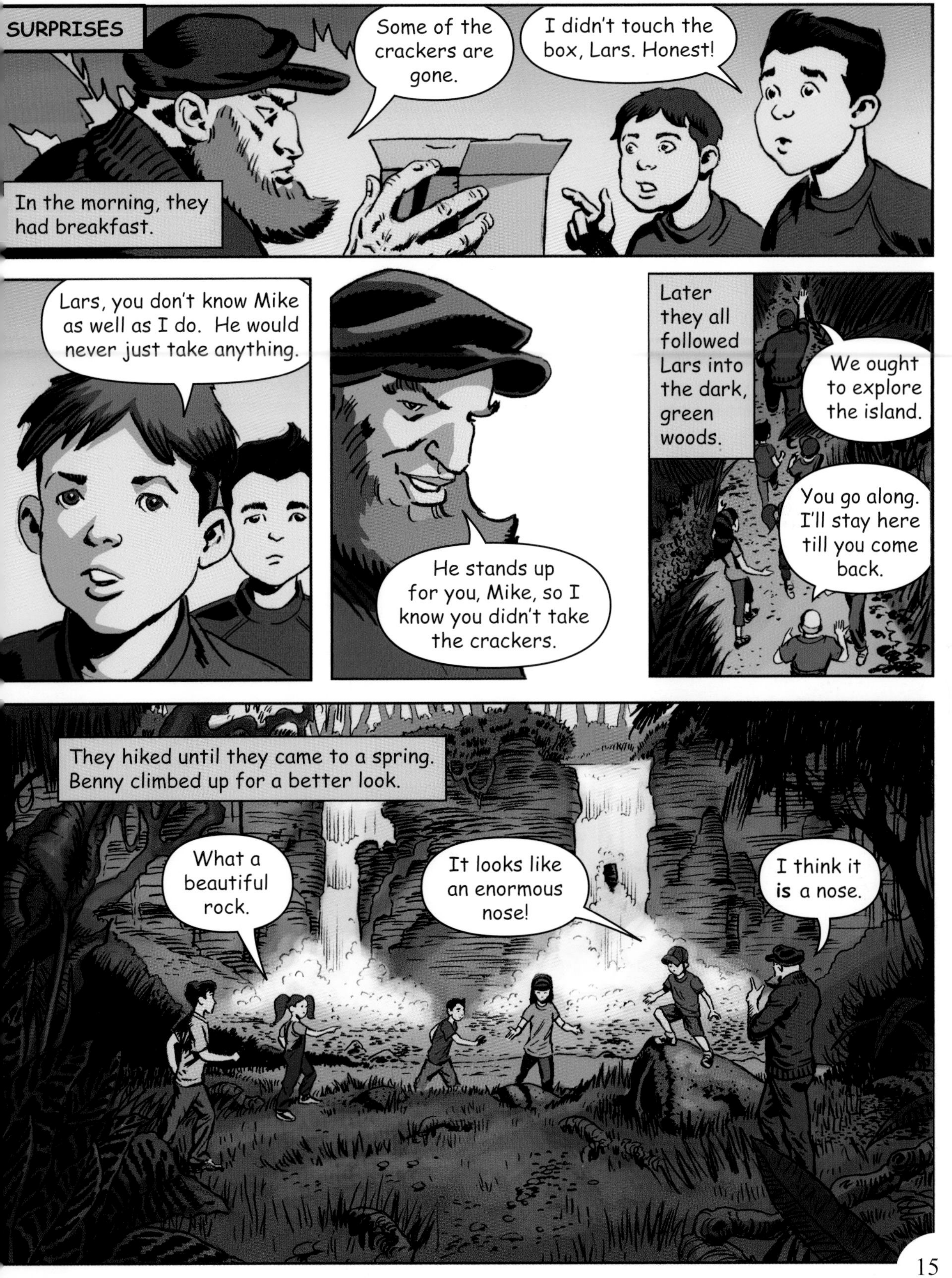
SURPRISES
In the morning, they had breakfast.
Some of the crackers are gone.
I didn't touch the box, Lars. Honest!
Lars, you don't know Mike as well as I do. He would never just take anything.
He stands up for you, Mike, so I know you didn't take the crackers.
Later they all followed Lars into the dark, green woods.
We ought to explore the island.
You go along. I'll stay here till you come back.
They hiked until they came to a spring. Benny climbed up for a better look.
What a beautiful rock.
It looks like an enormous nose!
I think it **is** a nose.

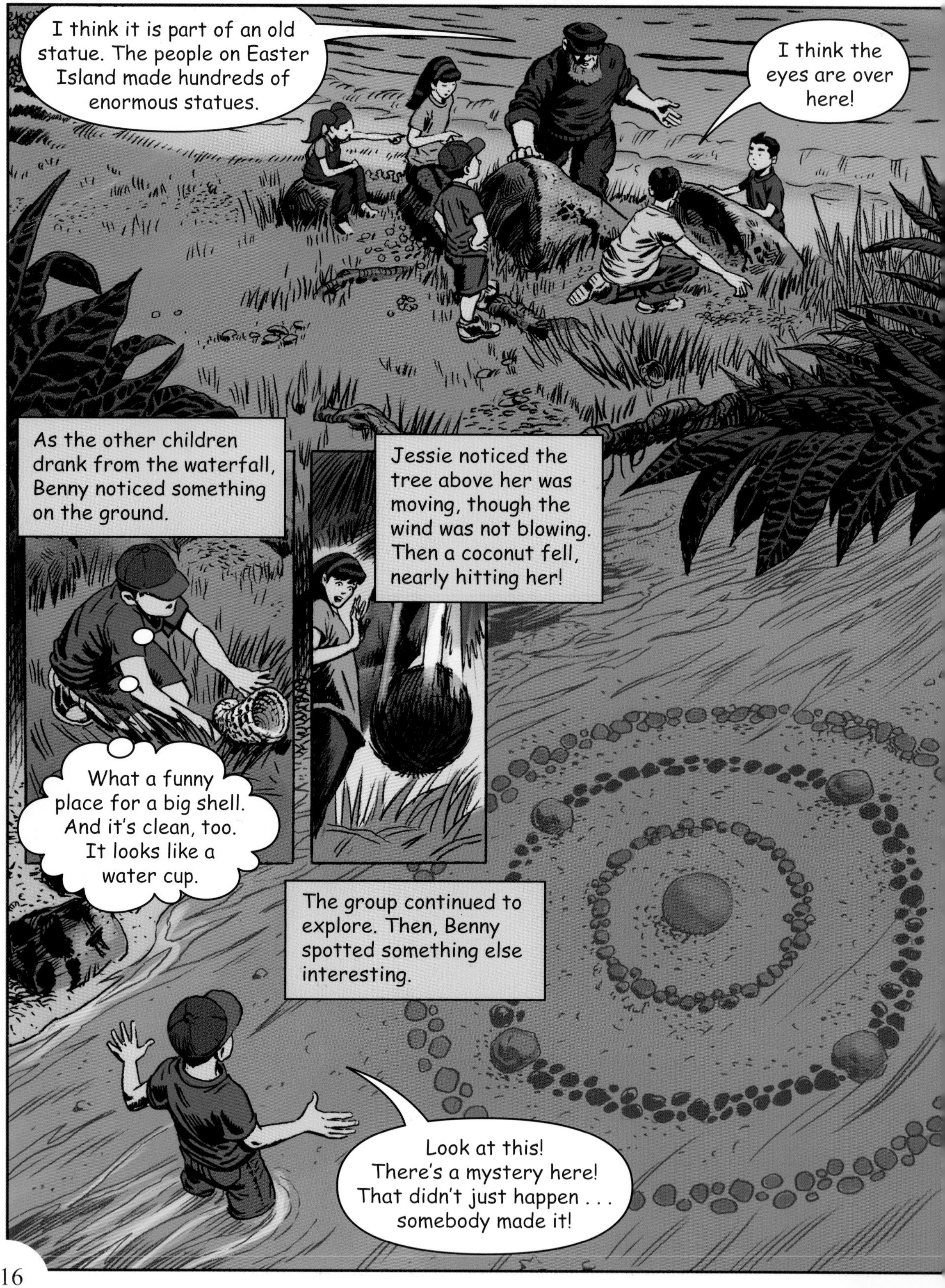
I think it is part of an old statue. The people on Easter Island made hundreds of enormous statues.
I think the eyes are over here!
As the other children drank from the waterfall, Benny noticed something on the ground.
What a funny place for a big shell. And it's clean, too. It looks like a water cup.
Jessie noticed the tree above her was moving, though the wind was not blowing. Then a coconut fell, nearly hitting her!
The group continued to explore. Then, Benny spotted something else interesting.
Look at this! There's a mystery here! That didn't just happen . . . somebody made it!

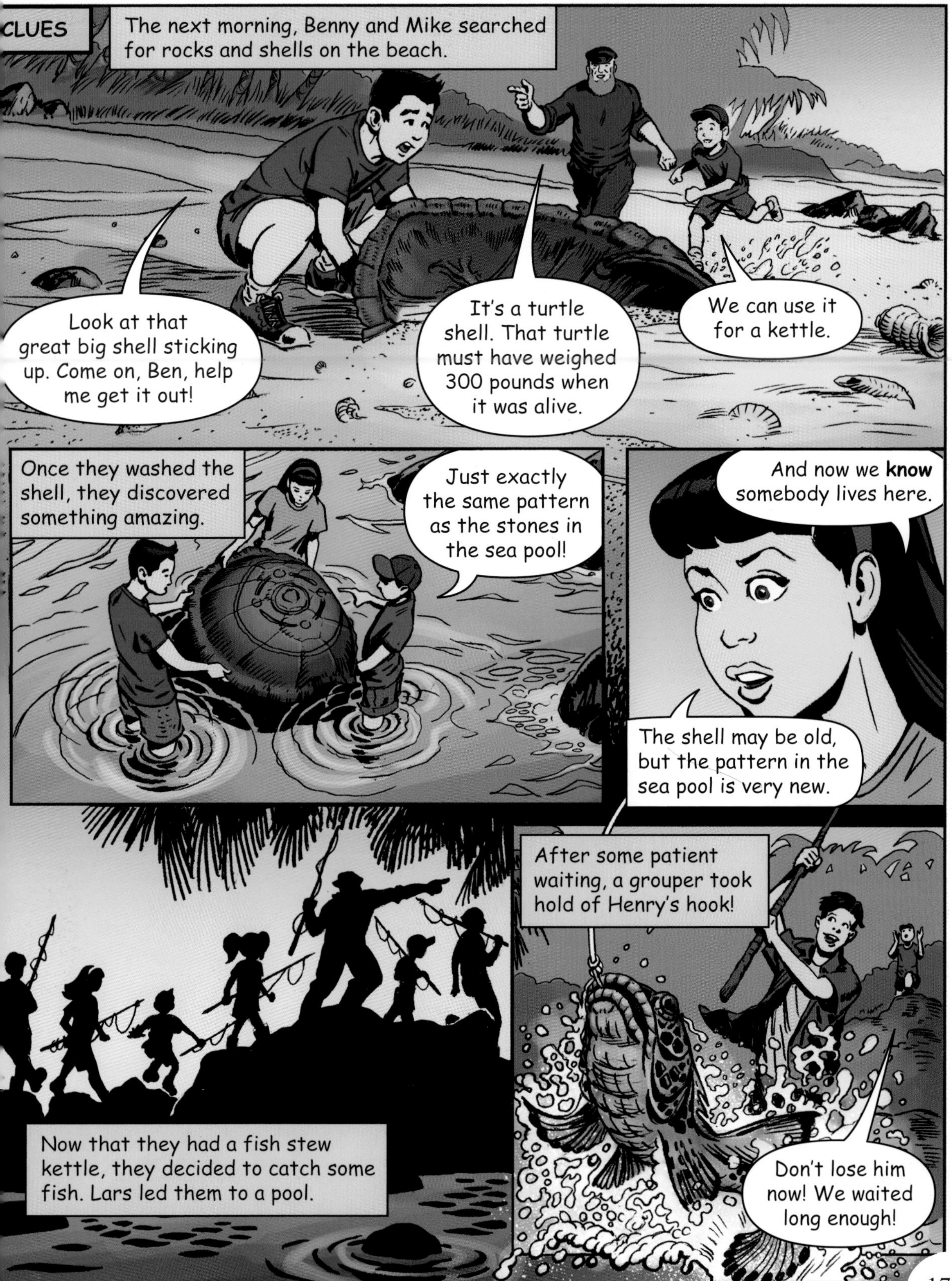

CLUES
The next morning, Benny and Mike searched for rocks and shells on the beach.
Look at that great big shell sticking up. Come on, Ben, help me get it out!
It's a turtle shell. That turtle must have weighed 300 pounds when it was alive.
We can use it for a kettle.
Once they washed the shell, they discovered something amazing.
Just exactly the same pattern as the stones in the sea pool!
And now we **know** somebody lives here.
The shell may be old, but the pattern in the sea pool is very new.
Now that they had a fish stew kettle, they decided to catch some fish. Lars led them to a pool.
After some patient waiting, a grouper took hold of Henry's hook!
Don't lose him now! We waited long enough!

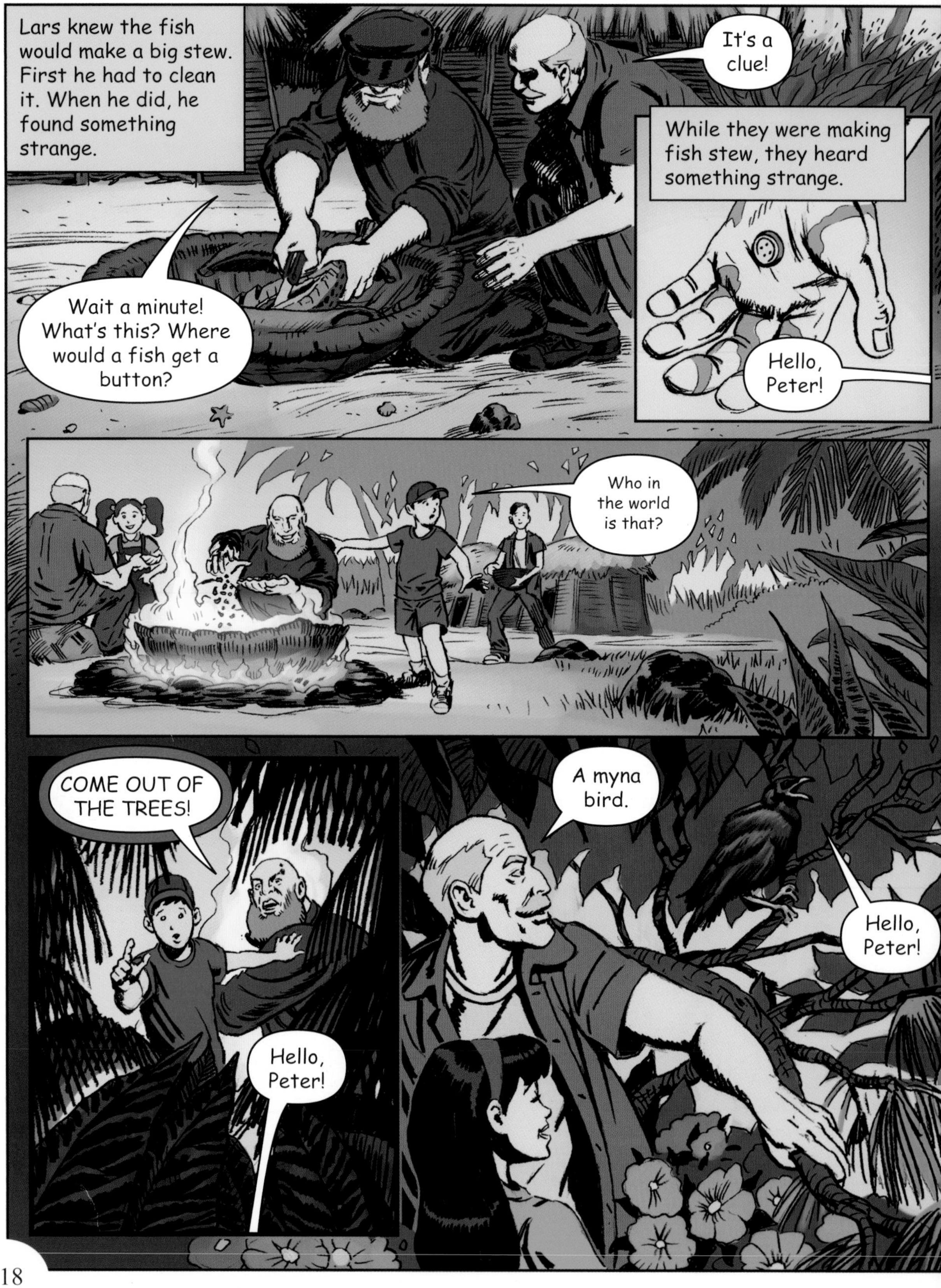

Lars knew the fish would make a big stew. First he had to clean it. When he did, he found something strange.
Wait a minute! What's this? Where would a fish get a button?
It's a clue!
While they were making fish stew, they heard something strange.
Hello, Peter!
Who in the world is that?
COME OUT OF THE TREES!
Hello, Peter!
A myna bird.
Hello, Peter!

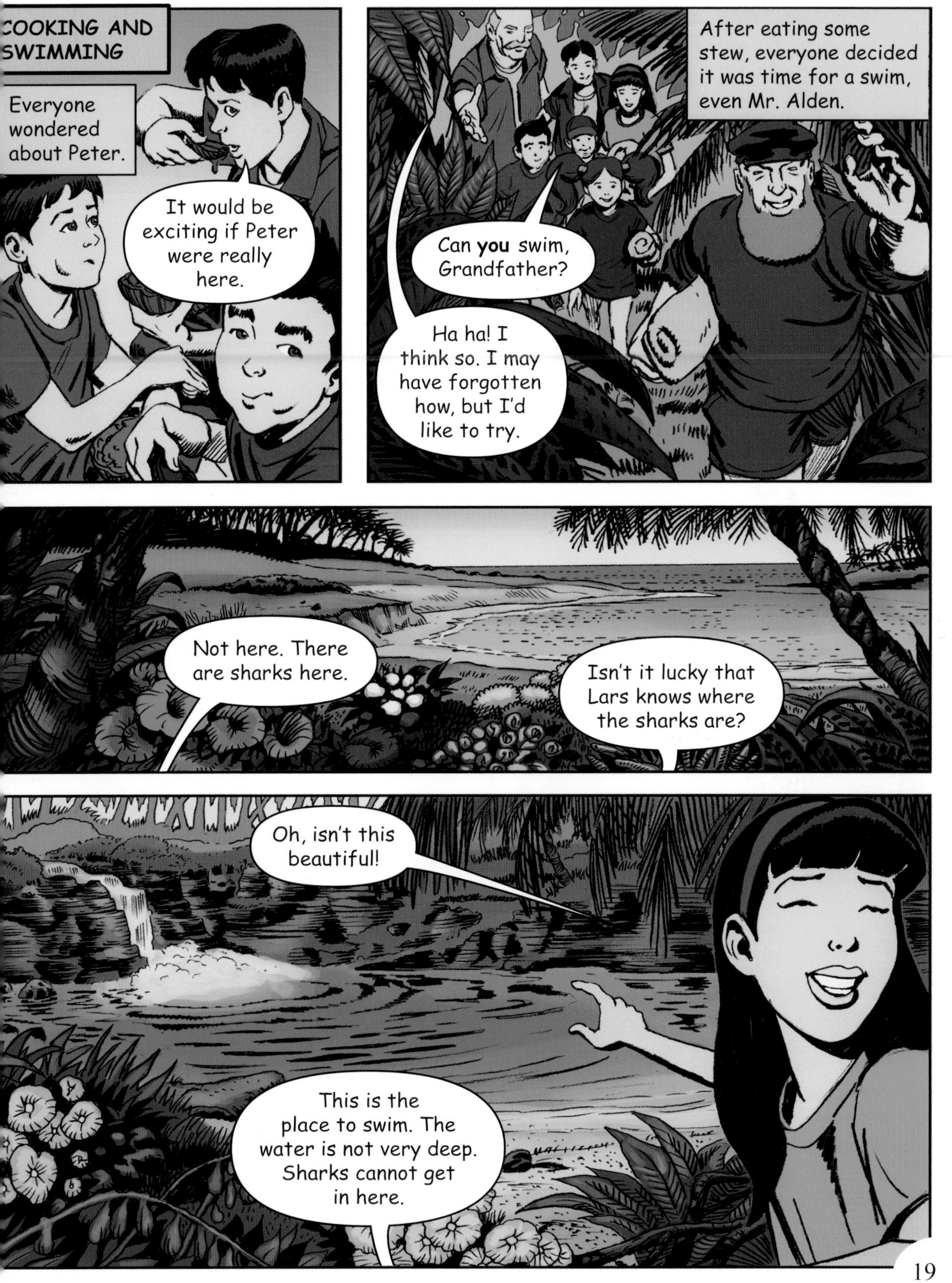
COOKING AND SWIMMING
Everyone wondered about Peter.
It would be exciting if Peter were really here.
After eating some stew, everyone decided it was time for a swim, even Mr. Alden.
Can **you** swim, Grandfather?
Ha ha! I think so. I may have forgotten how, but I'd like to try.
Not here. There are sharks here.
Isn't it lucky that Lars knows where the sharks are?
Oh, isn't this beautiful!
This is the place to swim. The water is not very deep. Sharks cannot get in here.

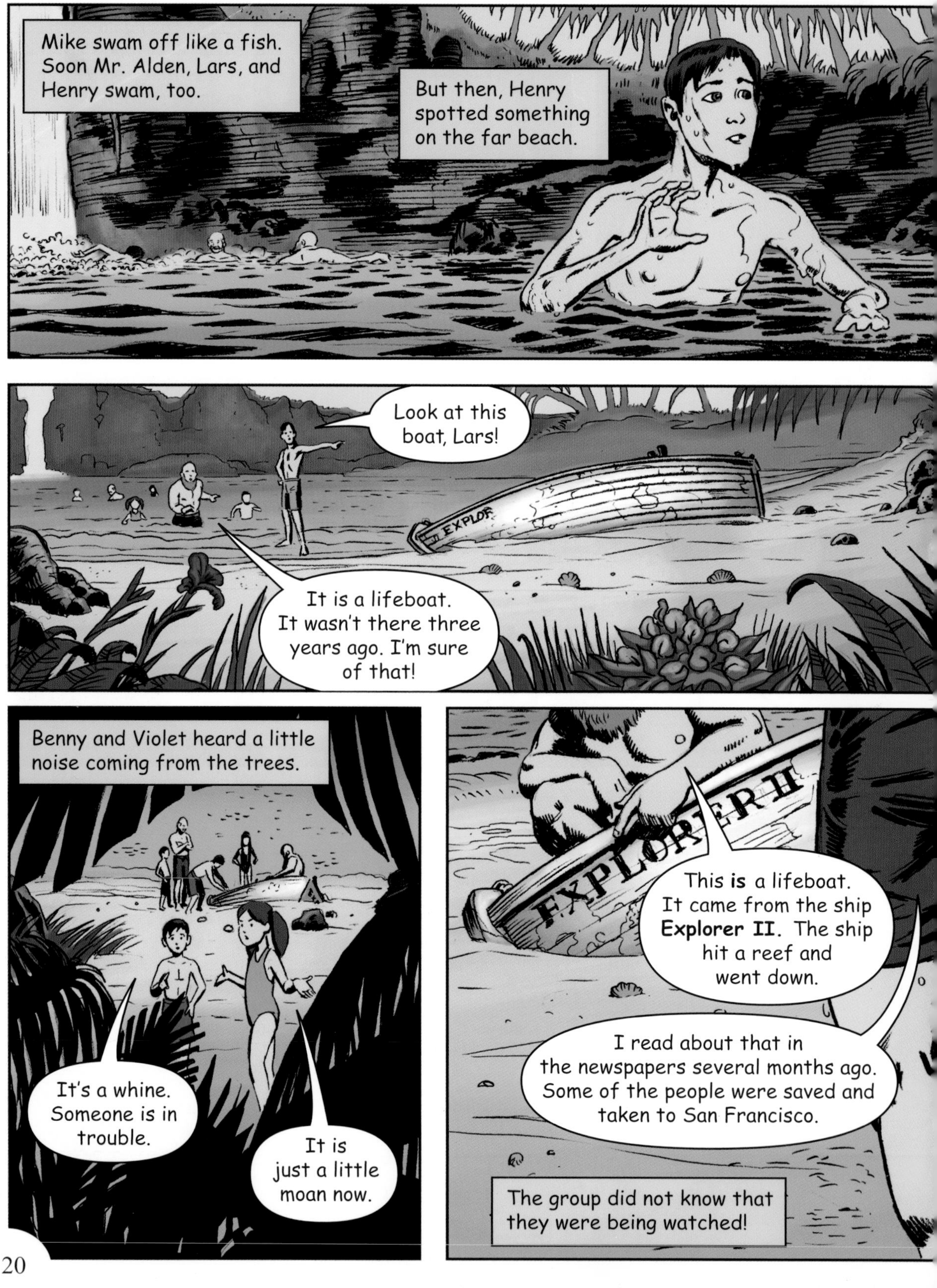

Mike swam off like a fish. Soon Mr. Alden, Lars, and Henry swam, too.
But then, Henry spotted something on the far beach.
Look at this boat, Lars!
EXPLOR
It is a lifeboat. It wasn't there three years ago. I'm sure of that!
Benny and Violet heard a little noise coming from the trees.
It's a whine. Someone is in trouble.
It is just a little moan now.
EXPLORER II
This **is** a lifeboat. It came from the ship **Explorer II.** The ship hit a reef and went down.
I read about that in the newspapers several months ago. Some of the people were saved and taken to San Francisco.
The group did not know that they were being watched!

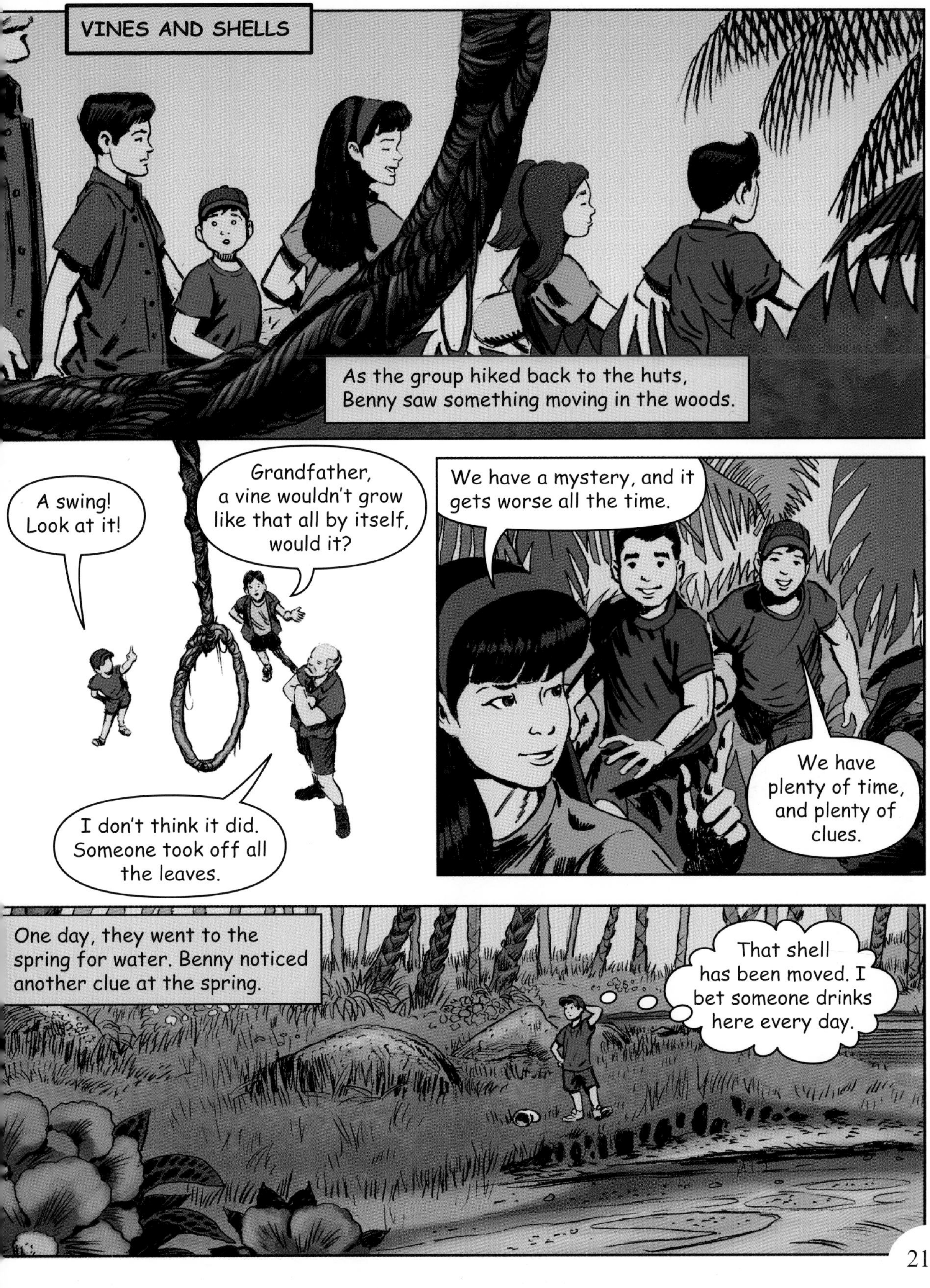
VINES AND SHELLS
As the group hiked back to the huts, Benny saw something moving in the woods.
A swing! Look at it!
Grandfather, a vine wouldn't grow like that all by itself, would it?
I don't think it did. Someone took off all the leaves.
We have a mystery, and it gets worse all the time.
We have plenty of time, and plenty of clues.
One day, they went to the spring for water. Benny noticed another clue at the spring.
That shell has been moved. I bet someone drinks here every day.

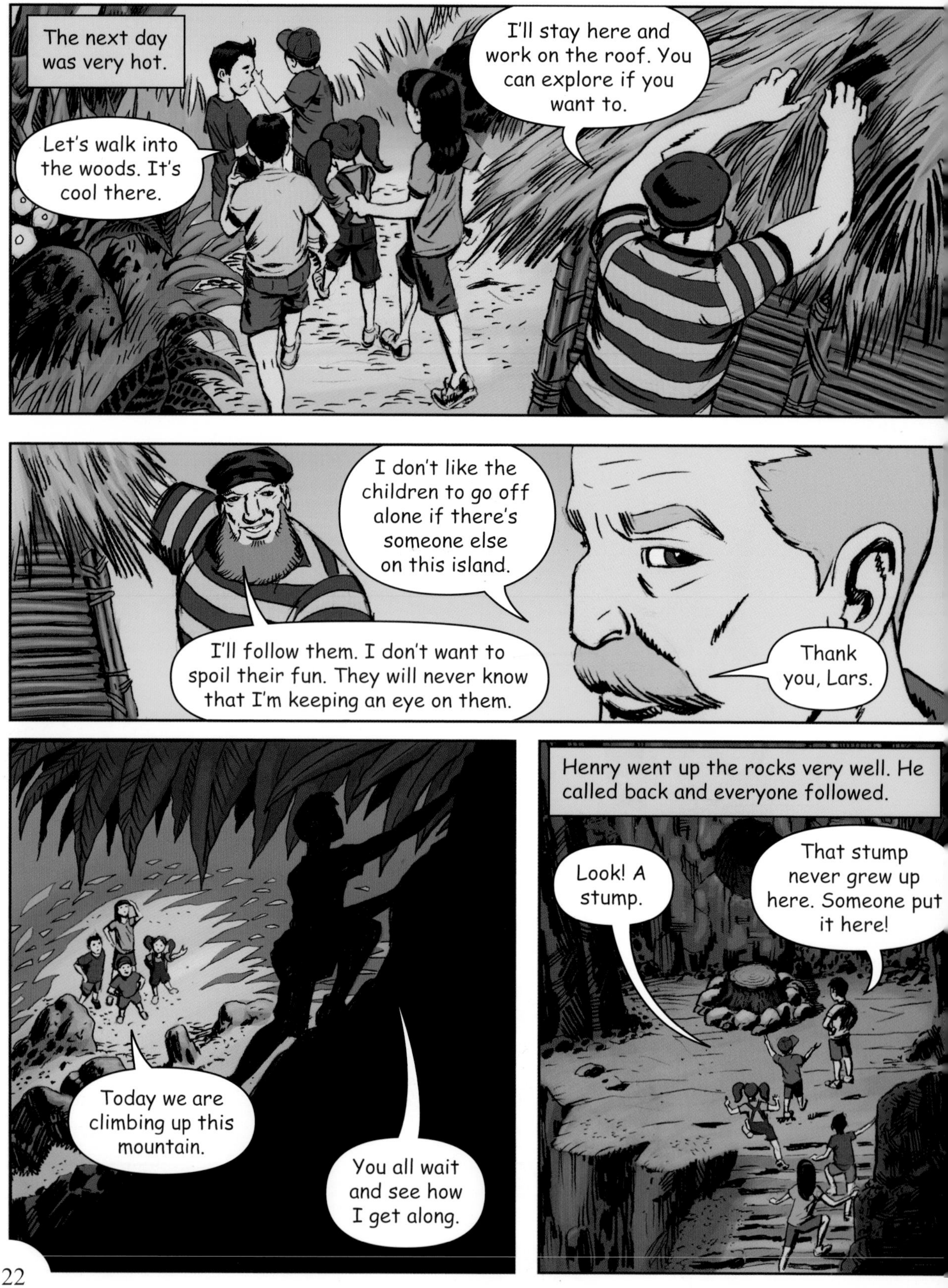

The next day was very hot.
Let's walk into the woods. It's cool there.
I'll stay here and work on the roof. You can explore if you want to.
I don't like the children to go off alone if there's someone else on this island.
I'll follow them. I don't want to spoil their fun. They will never know that I'm keeping an eye on them.
Thank you, Lars.
Today we are climbing up this mountain.
You all wait and see how I get along.
Henry went up the rocks very well. He called back and everyone followed.
Look! A stump.
That stump never grew up here. Someone put it here!

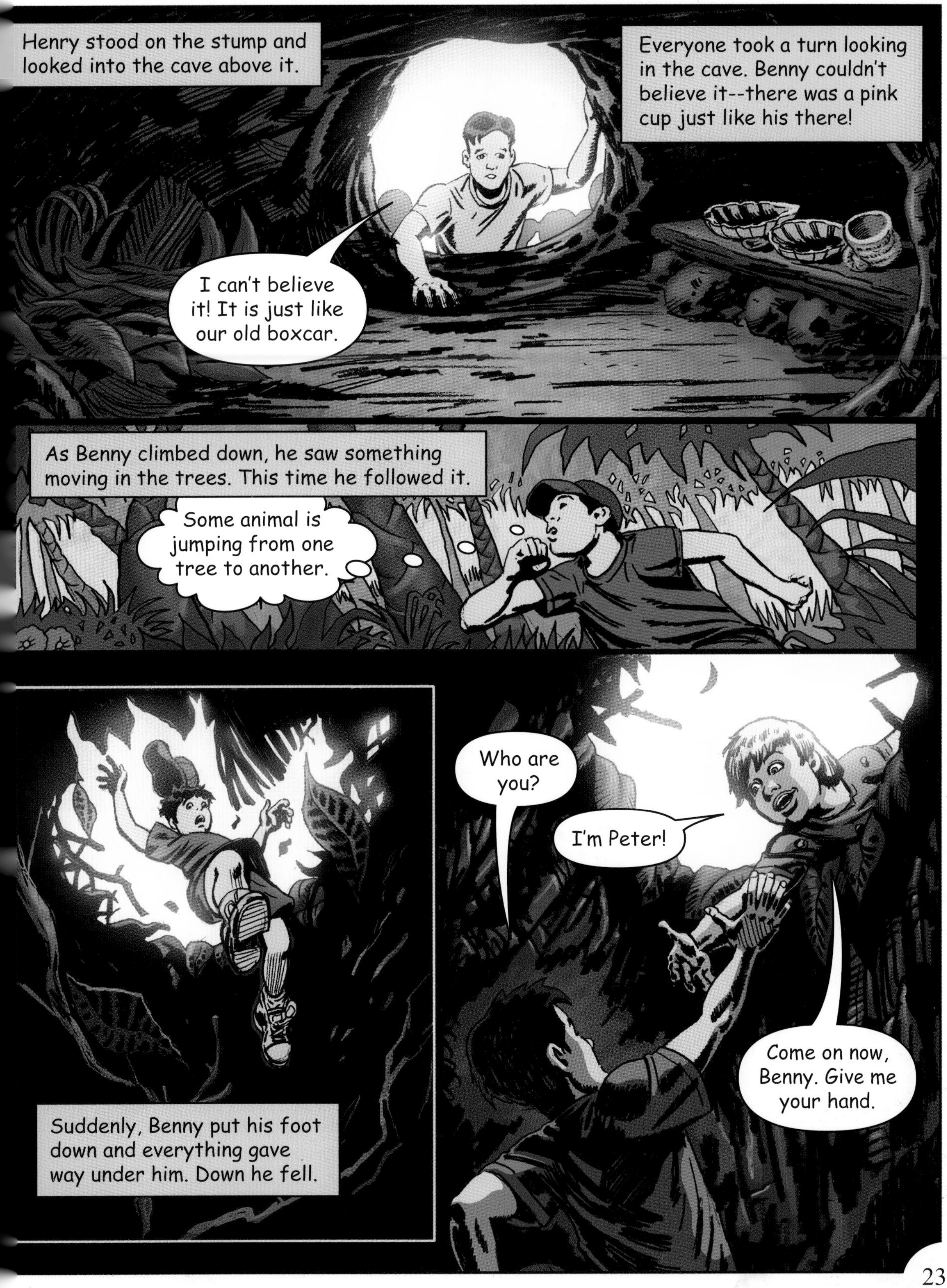
Henry stood on the stump and looked into the cave above it.
I can't believe it! It is just like our old boxcar.
Everyone took a turn looking in the cave. Benny couldn't believe it--there was a pink cup just like his there!
As Benny climbed down, he saw something moving in the trees. This time he followed it.
Some animal is jumping from one tree to another.
Suddenly, Benny put his foot down and everything gave way under him. Down he fell.
Who are you?
I'm Peter!
Come on now, Benny. Give me your hand.

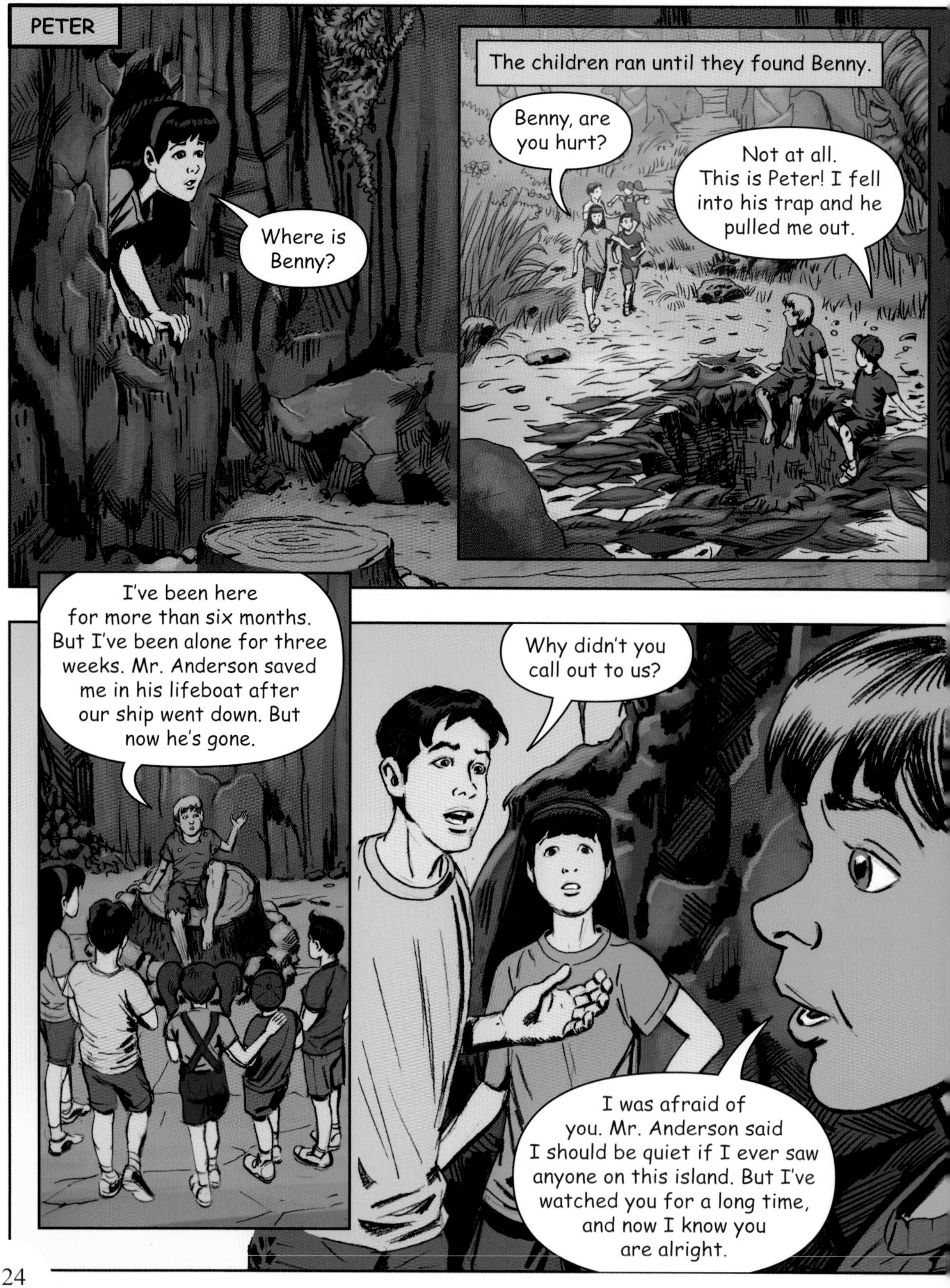
PETER
Where is Benny?
The children ran until they found Benny.
Benny, are you hurt?
Not at all. This is Peter! I fell into his trap and he pulled me out.
I've been here for more than six months. But I've been alone for three weeks. Mr. Anderson saved me in his lifeboat after our ship went down. But now he's gone.
Why didn't you call out to us?
I was afraid of you. Mr. Anderson said I should be quiet if I ever saw anyone on this island. But I've watched you for a long time, and now I know you are alright.

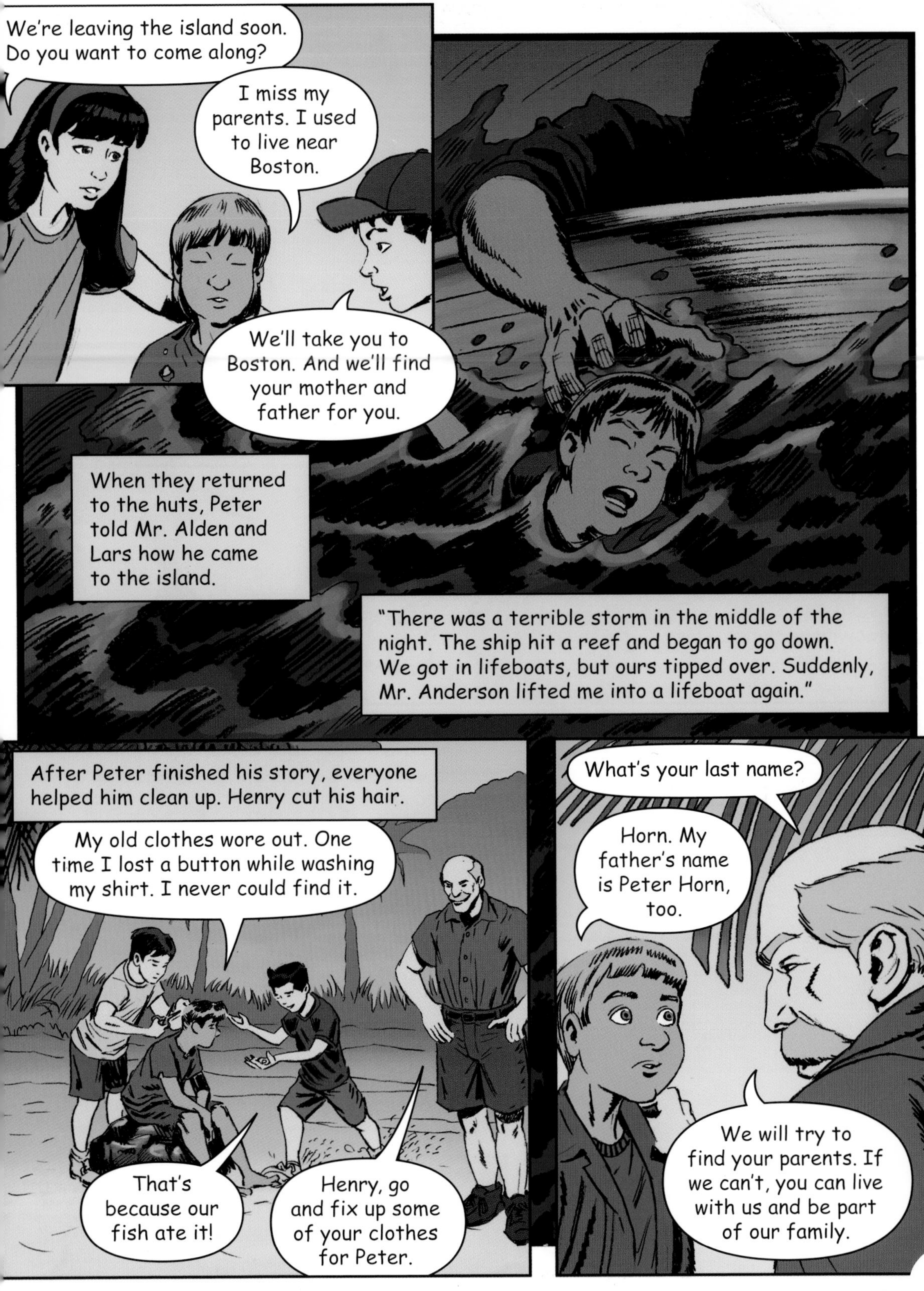

We're leaving the island soon. Do you want to come along?
I miss my parents. I used to live near Boston.
We'll take you to Boston. And we'll find your mother and father for you.
When they returned to the huts, Peter told Mr. Alden and Lars how he came to the island.
"There was a terrible storm in the middle of the night. The ship hit a reef and began to go down. We got in lifeboats, but ours tipped over. Suddenly, Mr. Anderson lifted me into a lifeboat again."
After Peter finished his story, everyone helped him clean up. Henry cut his hair.
My old clothes wore out. One time I lost a button while washing my shirt. I never could find it.
That's because our fish ate it!
Henry, go and fix up some of your clothes for Peter.
What's your last name?
Horn. My father's name is Peter Horn, too.
We will try to find your parents. If we can't, you can live with us and be part of our family.

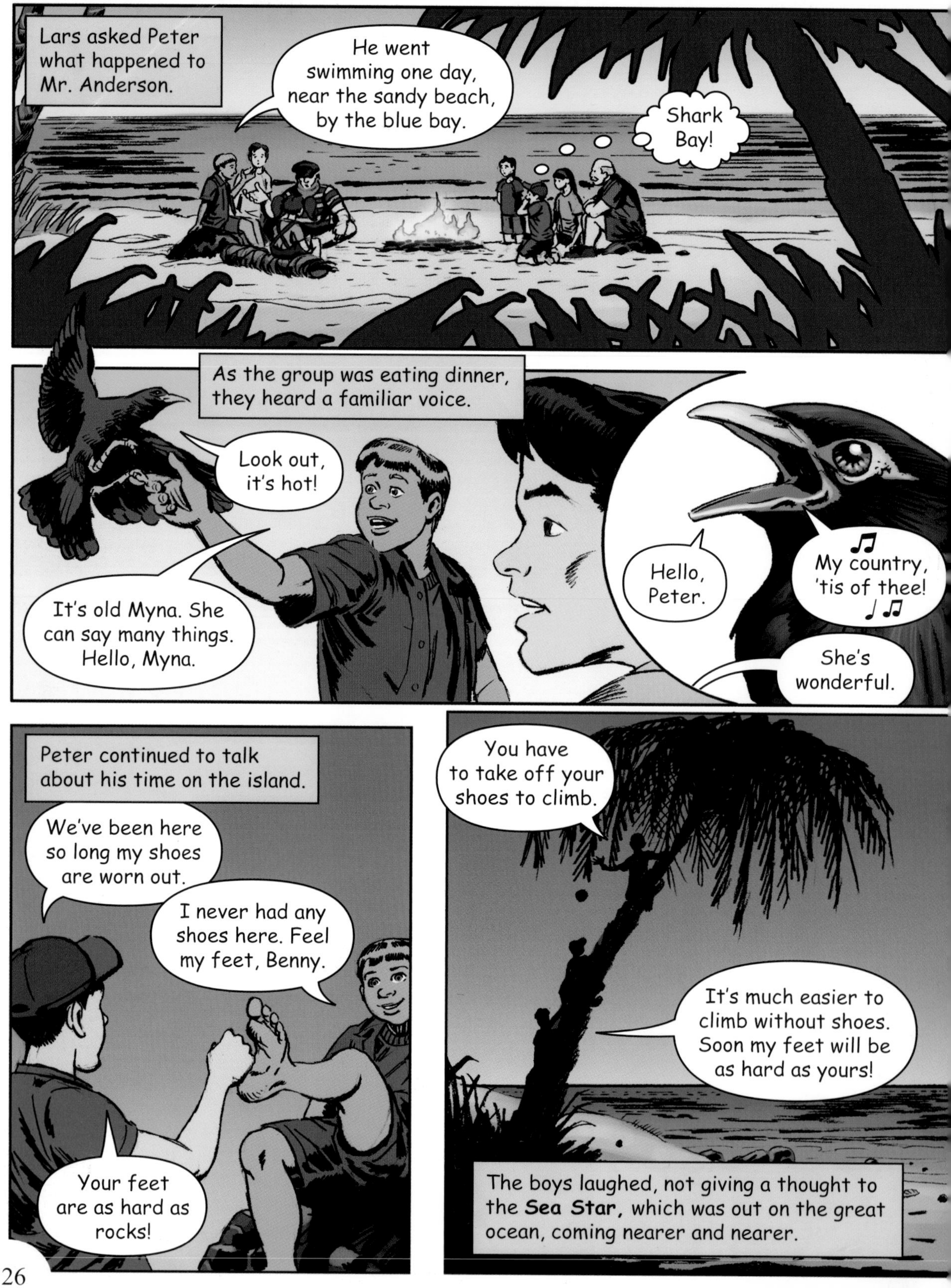
Lars asked Peter what happened to Mr. Anderson.
He went swimming one day, near the sandy beach, by the blue bay.
Shark Bay!
As the group was eating dinner, they heard a familiar voice.
Look out, it's hot!
It's old Myna. She can say many things. Hello, Myna.
Hello, Peter.
My country, 'tis of thee!
She's wonderful.
Peter continued to talk about his time on the island.
We've been here so long my shoes are worn out.
I never had any shoes here. Feel my feet, Benny.
Your feet are as hard as rocks!
You have to take off your shoes to climb.
It's much easier to climb without shoes. Soon my feet will be as hard as yours!
The boys laughed, not giving a thought to the **Sea Star**, which was out on the great ocean, coming nearer and nearer.

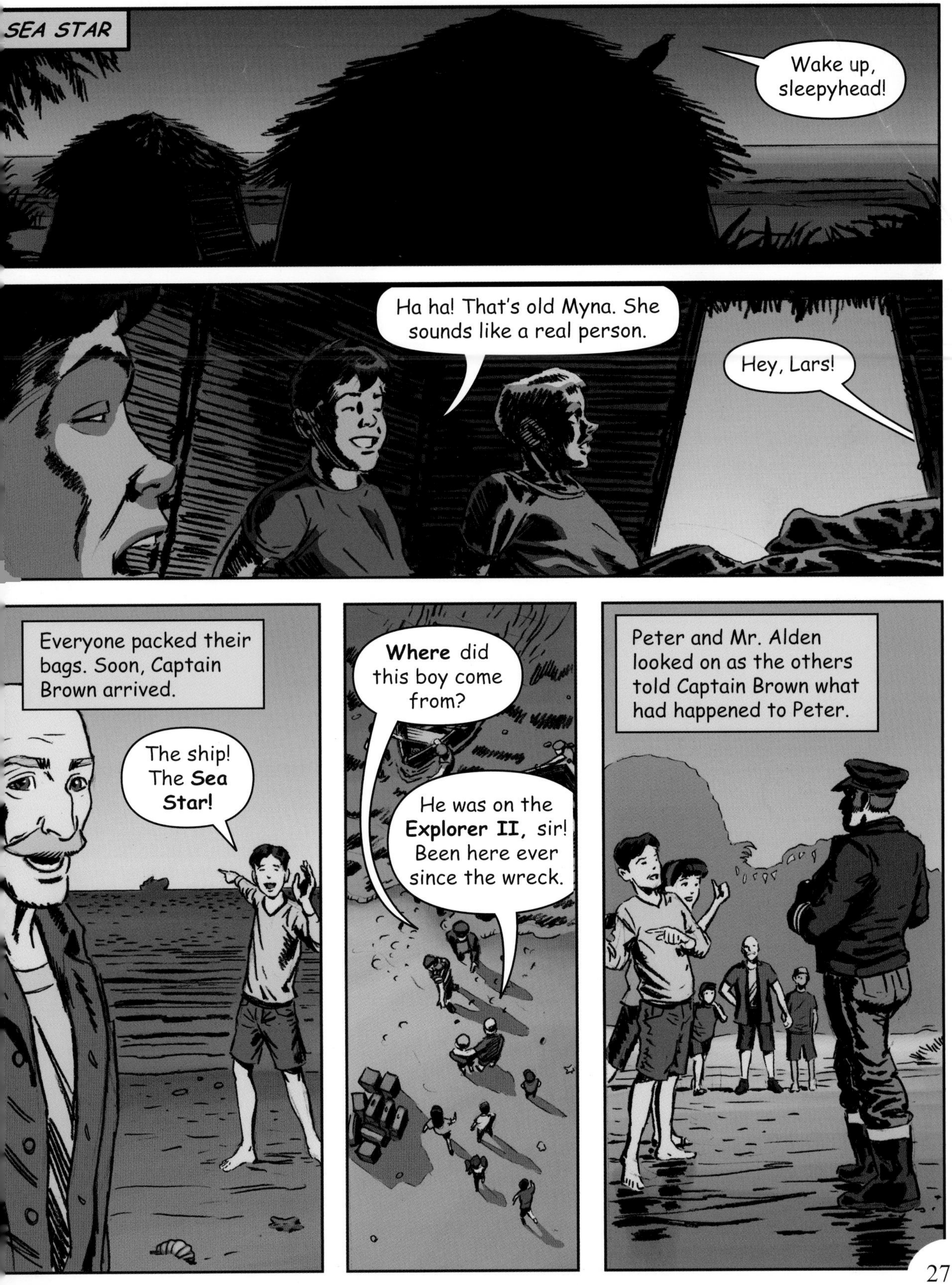
SEA STAR
Wake up, sleepyhead!
Ha ha! That's old Myna. She sounds like a real person.
Hey, Lars!
Everyone packed their bags. Soon, Captain Brown arrived.
The ship! The **Sea Star!**
Where did this boy come from?
He was on the **Explorer II,** sir! Been here ever since the wreck.
Peter and Mr. Alden looked on as the others told Captain Brown what had happened to Peter.

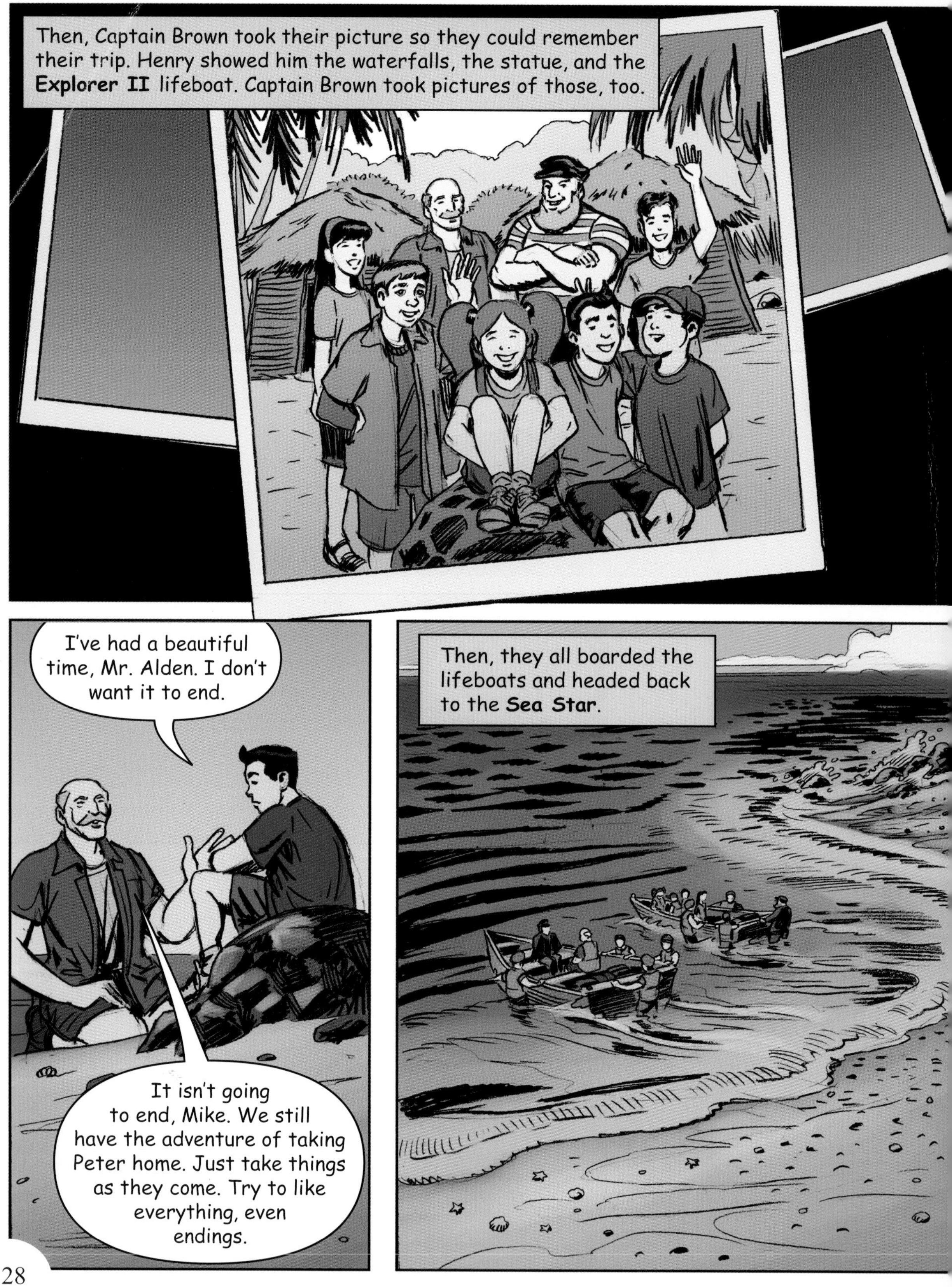
Then, Captain Brown took their picture so they could remember their trip. Henry showed him the waterfalls, the statue, and the **Explorer II** lifeboat. Captain Brown took pictures of those, too.
I've had a beautiful time, Mr. Alden. I don't want it to end.
It isn't going to end, Mike. We still have the adventure of taking Peter home. Just take things as they come. Try to like everything, even endings.
Then, they all boarded the lifeboats and headed back to the **Sea Star**.

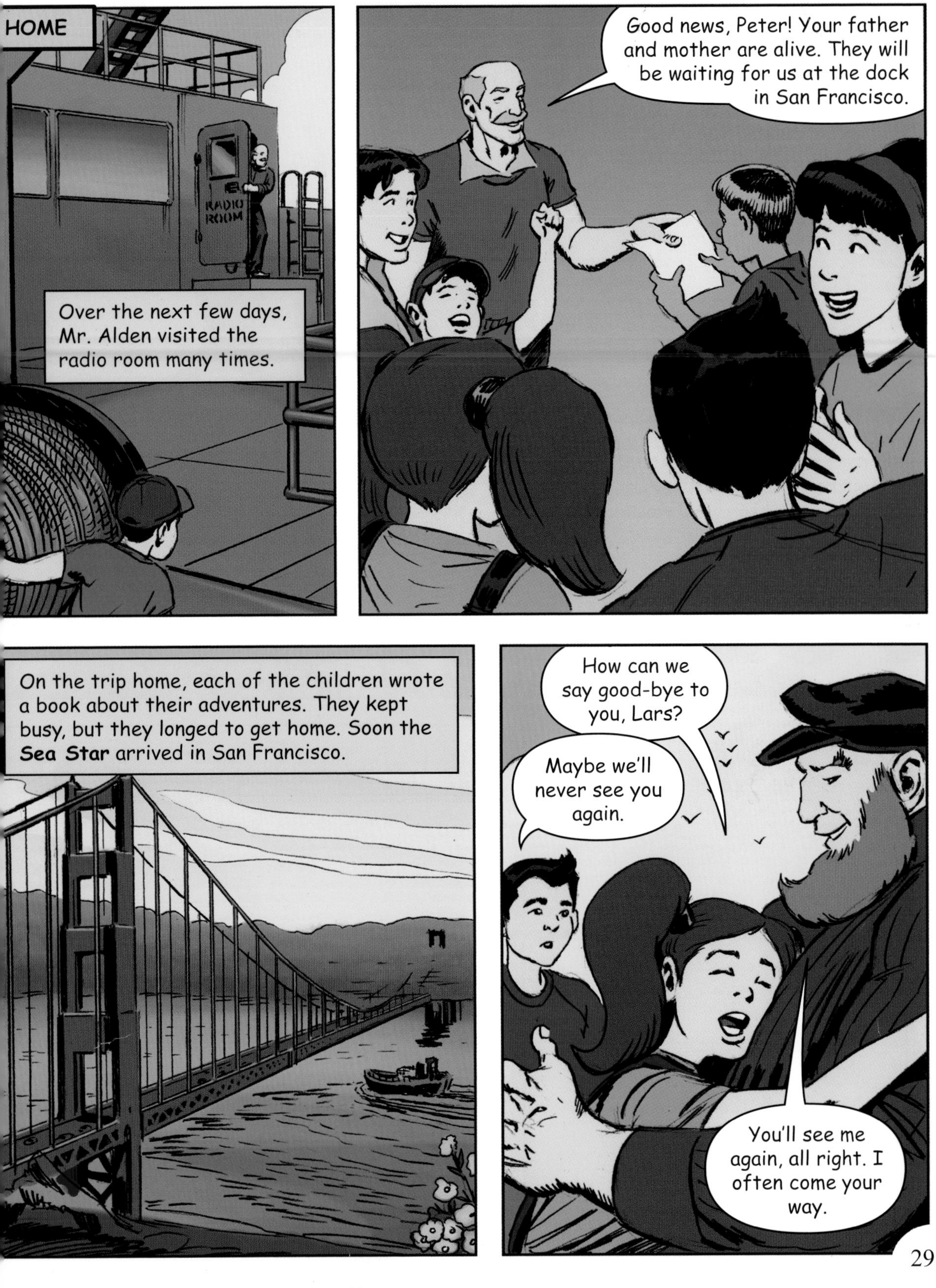
HOME
Over the next few days, Mr. Alden visited the radio room many times.
RADIO ROOM
Good news, Peter! Your father and mother are alive. They will be waiting for us at the dock in San Francisco.
On the trip home, each of the children wrote a book about their adventures. They kept busy, but they longed to get home. Soon the **Sea Star** arrived in San Francisco.
How can we say good-bye to you, Lars?
Maybe we'll never see you again.
You'll see me again, all right. I often come your way.

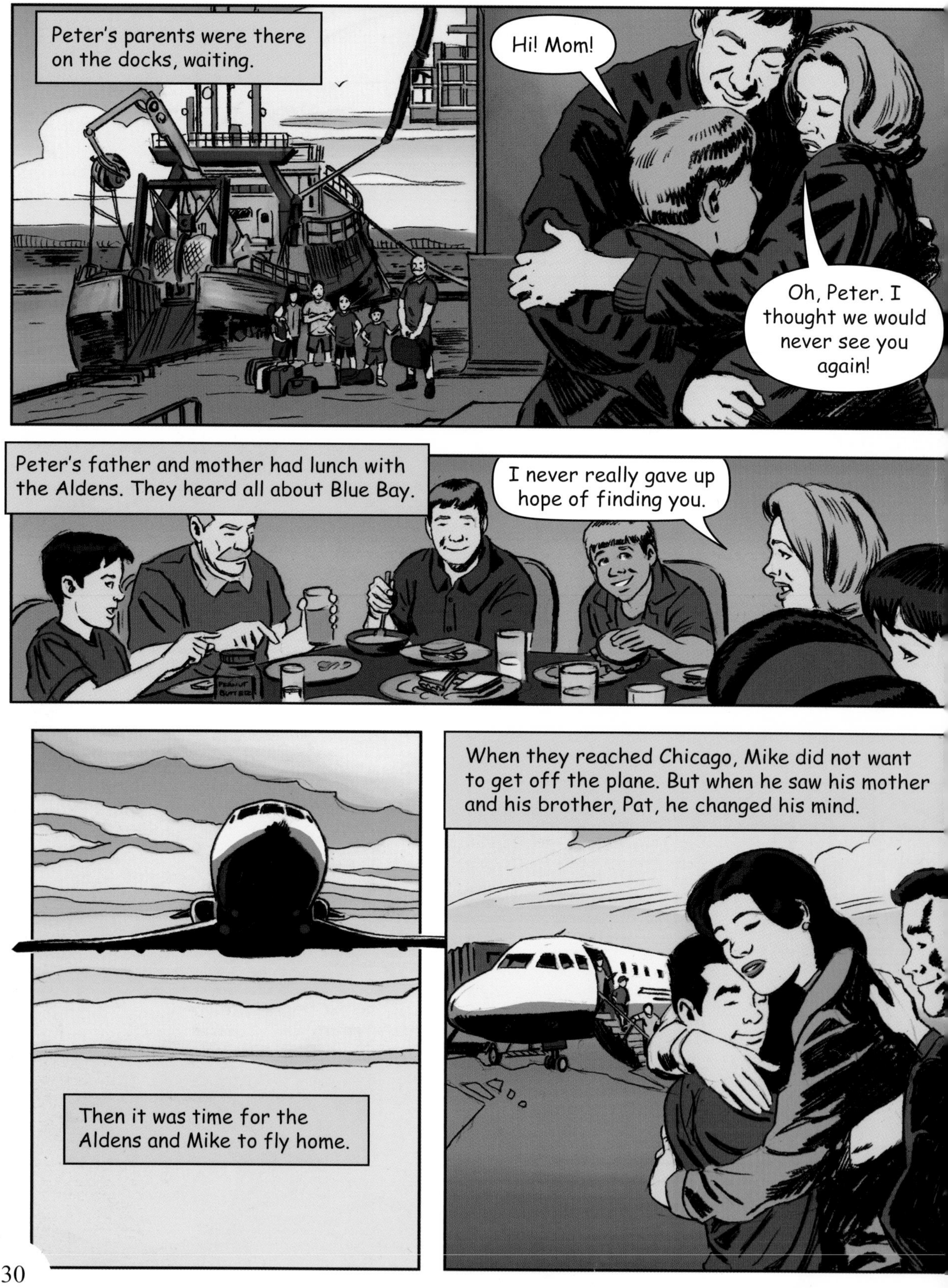
Peter's parents were there on the docks, waiting.
Hi! Mom!
Oh, Peter. I thought we would never see you again!
Peter's father and mother had lunch with the Aldens. They heard all about Blue Bay.
I never really gave up hope of finding you.
Then it was time for the Aldens and Mike to fly home.
When they reached Chicago, Mike did not want to get off the plane. But when he saw his mother and his brother, Pat, he changed his mind.

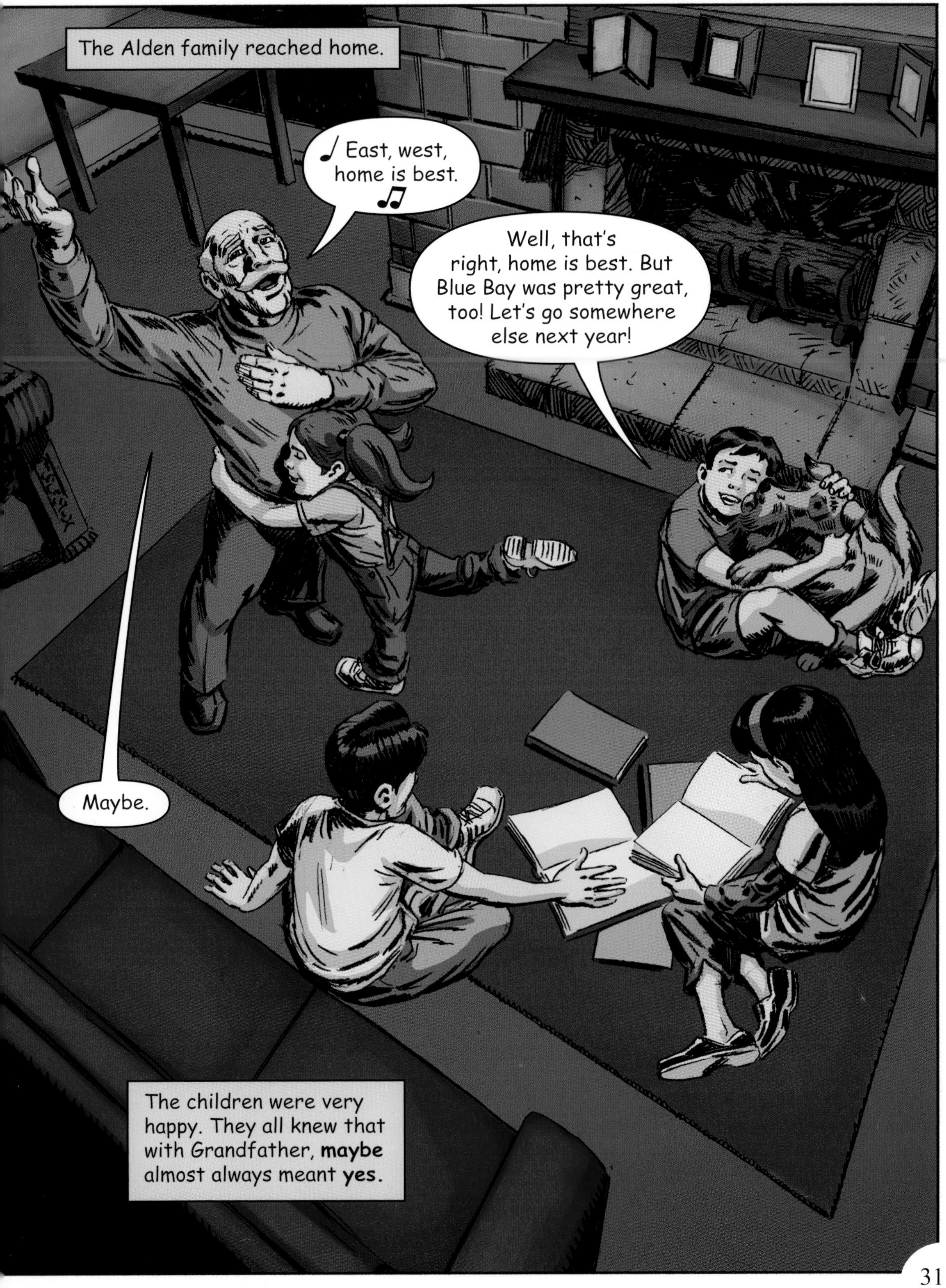
The Alden family reached home.
East, west, home is best.
Well, that's right, home is best. But Blue Bay was pretty great, too! Let's go somewhere else next year!
Maybe.
The children were very happy. They all knew that with Grandfather, **maybe** almost always meant **yes**.

ABOUT THE CREATOR

Gertrude Chandler Warner was born on April 16, 1890, in Putnam, Connecticut. In 1918, Warner began teaching at Israel Putnam School. As a teacher, she discovered that many readers who liked an exciting story could not find books that were both easy and fun to read. She decided to try to meet this need. In 1942, *The Boxcar Children* was published for these readers.

Warner drew on her own experience to write *The Boxcar Children.* As a child she spent hours watching trains go by on the tracks near her family home. She often dreamed about what it would be like to live in a caboose or freight car—just as the Alden children do.

When readers asked for more Alden adventures, Warner began additional stories. While the mystery element is central to each of the books, she never thought of them as strictly juvenile mysteries. She liked to stress the Aldens' independence. Henry, Jessie, Violet, and Benny go about most of their adventures with as little adult supervision as possible—something that delights young readers.

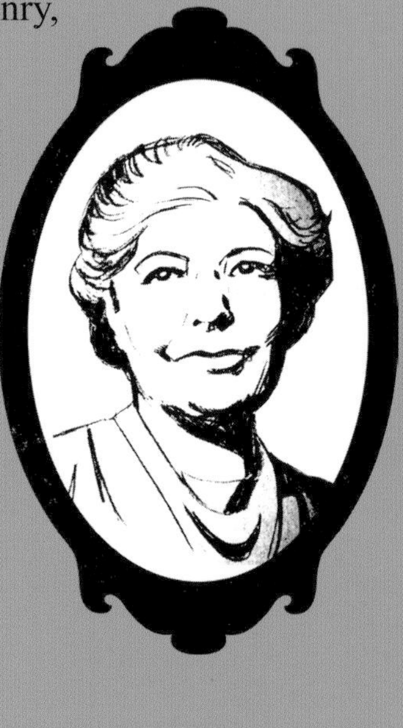

During her lifetime, Warner received hundreds of letters from fans as she continued the Aldens' adventures, writing nineteen Boxcar Children books in all. After her death in 1979, her publisher, Albert Whitman and Company, carried on Warner's vision. Today, the Boxcar Children series has more than 100 books.